Do the World a Favour

***Other Five Star titles
by Mat Coward:***

Up and Down
In and Out

Do the World a Favour

and Other Stories

Mat Coward

Five Star • Waterville, Maine

First Edition
First Printing: January 2003

Published in 2003 in conjunction with
Tekno Books and Ed Gorman.

Set in 11 pt. Plantin by Al Chase.

Printed in the United States on permanent paper.

Library of Congress Cataloging-in-Publication Data

Coward, Mat.
    Do the world a favour, and other stories / Mat Coward.
        p. cm.—(Five Star first edition mystery series)
    ISBN 0-7862-4313-9 (hc : alk. paper)
    1. Detective and mystery stories, English.   I. Title.
II. Series.
PR6053.O955 D6 2003
823'.914—dc21   2002035944

Do the World a Favour

Do the World a Favour

and Other Stories

Introduction by Ian Rankin	9
History Repeats Itself, and It Doesn't Even Say Pardon	11
No Night by Myself	22
The Set-Up Man	41
The Shortest Distance	48
Do the World a Favour	63
Not a Minute on the Day	72
Famous for One Thing	87
Nowhere To Be Found	96
Breathe In	116
But Poor Men Pay for All	121
Tomorrow's Villain	143
Bits	161
Old Sultan	178
Twelve of the Little Buggers	192

Introduction

by Ian Rankin

Mat Coward has an expert's appreciation of the finer points of the good short story. His characterizations are visual and immediate in the space of only a few lines; we feel we really know these people. He tells a good story, too, one that grips you, entertains you, and makes you think. He can write comedy, tragedy, history—and sometimes all three in a single tale. He writes about cops as convincingly as he does criminals. He writes about ordinary people plunged into danger and psychosis. He invokes the guilty laugh, the thoughtful smile. In fact, I'm forced to admit it: he's just possibly the best writer of short stories working in the crime world today.

Read something like "No Night By Myself" and you'll see what I'm talking about: it's got pathos and humour and tension to spare. You're never sure which way it's going to go, right up until the ending. You feel for the characters and their shared dilemma. You *feel* for this crazy man who's invaded the family's peaceful Christmas. Just one of many very special stories in here. Even in the nastiest tales—and Coward can do "nasty" (try "Breathe In" or "Do The World A Favour")—there's a core of humanity to the characters, an understanding by the author of our basic struggle to defeat those demons within us. This is what Coward brings to the form; it makes his work worth savouring.

I love short stories. A much-maligned form, I know. It's as if, being short, they must lack substance. Yes, like a 20-

minute Rick Wakeman track has to be better than Motown. But short stories have immediacy, and the best ones linger in the mind. Mat Coward's stories resemble distilled novels. I can imagine some writers stretching one of these taut tales into two-hundred pages of prose . . . and the reader wouldn't have learned anything new from all that extra length. I remember a writer telling me, back in the days when I was struggling to become a writer myself, that he liked short stories because he could write one in an afternoon. I didn't say anything, but I did draw a deep breath, because back then it took me a week to write even the shortest piece. I would ponder, delete and tweak; go back to the beginning . . . Mat Coward's stories have the feel of effortlessness to them. It's the sort of thing that only comes with knowledge and love of the form . . . along with immense hard work. He's done the world a favour by writing them; you'll be doing yourself a favour by reading them.

So sit back, tense up, and enjoy.

Ian Rankin
Edinburgh, 2001

HISTORY REPEATS ITSELF,

AND IT DOESN'T EVEN SAY PARDON

Before becoming a north London copper, Colin Mann had been a south London villain.

Not many people knew this. Indeed, until yesterday, Colin would have said that nobody else knew it. Now, however, he knew that at least one other person did know, and that, of course, was a problem which needed to be sorted.

At the end of roll call, at the start of the shift, Colin caught PC Dunne as he was leaving the room. "You're in the area car, Nigel."

"Yes, Skip."

"I'll come with you. I want a word."

"Right, Skip. Great."

They walked out to the vehicle bay. Nigel Dunne kept looking at his sergeant, then looking away again. Colin said nothing, just kept thinking. He'd been a policeman for eleven years; he liked it. He thought he was quite good at it. He liked the pay; he liked the work. He didn't like coppers much, but you couldn't have everything. If it was possible, he wanted to stay in the job, stay and get his pension. He liked the way that, in the job, if you had a problem—you sorted it. That's what you were good at, if you were any good at all.

Once they were in the car, belted up, ready to go, Colin said, "Drive to the Shaw Estate. We'll have a chat."

"Yes, Sarge." The boy didn't look worried, Colin thought, he looked—what? Excited. As if the sergeant were

11

about to stand him a treat.

"Pull up over here. We'll sit here for a while."

They sat for a while. Colin just watching Dunne out of the corner of his eye, not surreptitiously, but not obviously. Dunne didn't even glance at Colin. He stared straight ahead, through the windscreen, and played his fingers back and forth along the steering wheel, like a pianist doing exercises. He looked very young, and very happy.

"So, how old are you, Nigel?"

Nigel spun his head round to face Colin, eager and fresh, his face shining in the urban twilight. "Twenty-one, Sarge." He made it sound like a boast, or a promise. "I've only been in two years, I was at college before that. College boy!"

"What were you studying?" He was genuinely curious. He couldn't see PC Dunne as graduate-entry.

"No, you know, just GCSEs, A Levels. I got French. Good that, handy for holidays."

"So you're a bright lad. You're not just another plonk, like the rest of us."

"Nothing like that, Skip, honest. I wish I'd joined earlier, tell you the truth. I just never thought of it until the recruitment stuff came round, at college."

Colin brought out a packet of cigarettes, lit one, then offered them to Dunne. Dunne didn't smoke, but he took one anyway, accepted a light, then held his head at an angle so the smoke wouldn't get in his eyes.

"What you said to me yesterday, Nigel. In the canteen."

"What was that, Skip?" He wanted to hear the exact words, from his sergeant's mouth. He'd taken ages working them out just right, and now he wanted to hear them, hear how good they sounded. How well he'd done.

"You said you knew where I grew up. You knew what I did before I joined the force."

"That's right, Sarge. I do."

Colin blew smoke in the young cop's face, blew it right into his eyes, in a fine, hard stream, and said, "I worked for my sister's husband, delivering motor parts. We had a van."

"No, no you didn't." Nigel shook his head, kept on shaking it, not in denial, but in complicity. Little foams of spit gathered at the corners of his mouth. "I know you were a driver, but you didn't drive a van. Not delivering parts, you didn't. No you never." Grinning like a dog.

Colin ground his cigarette out on the side window, thoroughly and violently, trying to make it look like he wasn't really content to be doing such violence to a fag end, but a fag end'd do, for now, until something better came along. "That's what it says on my record."

"I know what it was like back then, Sarge. Early eighties, it wasn't like now, it was dead easy to get in the job then. They were desperate. Dead easy for a man like you. A clever, hard man like you. No sweat."

"You married, Nigel?"

"No, Sarge. Sort of . . ." He stopped.

"You've got a girl?"

"I wouldn't want the job to know. I mean, not you Skip, you're different, I don't mind you knowing. She's older than me. You've met her, actually. In the Fat Duck, when Mr. Johnson retired. She was with me then. You said hello."

"We can't leave it like this, Nigel. You understand?" He wasn't going to say, *"What do you want from me?"* He wasn't going to say, *"What's your price?"* You couldn't start paying people, not after eleven years.

"Sure, Sarge. What are we going to do?"

"I'm going to do this," said Colin. He reached across to take the keys out of the ignition, got out of the patrol car, walked off into the darkness and disappeared. These are my

13

skills, he thought, this is what I can do: arresting people, hurting people, and disappearing. It had always proved enough, so far.

He walked around the rest of the night, ignoring the shouts from his radio, just walking. He called in once, to say he was going off air for a bit, and he knew what they'd think in the CAD room—he'd got a bird. That was all right, he never gave them any trouble, they'd cover for him just this once.

It wasn't what Nigel Dunne wanted from him—whatever that might turn out to be—that worried him. He didn't care what the price was, didn't have to care, because he wasn't going to pay it. It was Dunne knowing—simple as that. He couldn't have anyone knowing. It would have to be sorted, obviously.

He'd only ever killed one person. That man, too, had been a blackmailer of sorts, and if he had told what he knew, the people Colin ran with then would have killed Colin. So Colin had killed him. And then disappeared.

That was all right. He didn't like it, he wasn't a nutter, but it was all right. If it was justified.

Around midnight, he found a park bench and sat on it, lit his last cigarette. He liked being a copper. He'd never much liked being a villain; he could do either, certainly, do one as well as the other, probably, but he knew which he preferred. And this problem . . . it did have to be sorted. No way round that.

But first he needed to know how Nigel had found out. That was important. The boy was too young to have recognized him, had never lived in south London, anyway. Colin had checked. Which meant—*Oh, Christ!*—which meant there had to be more than one person who knew about him.

Just how many fucking problems were there? And was he up to sorting them all?

★ ★ ★ ★ ★

He should have brought a book, he thought. One of those magazines with all puzzles in them, crosswords, anagrams. Usually, on an observation, you could chat with the others, pass the time telling old jokes. But today, in his own car on his Saturday off, parked across the street from PC Dunne's house, he was bored out of his mind. And then he saw her.

Coming out of the house. Stopping to put the milk in, then walking on down the street, towards the Tube station. Going shopping, perhaps, or to the hairdressers. Going to visit her mum, maybe.

No, not visiting her mum, definitely not; her mum was long dead. Because he knew her now, now that he had some idea what he was looking for, knew where he knew her from. Remembered her history, and realised how she might have remembered his, across eleven years, not put off by the grey hair, the new name, the uniform.

Nigel opened the door to his second ring of the bell. "Skip! Great, great to see you, come in. You've just missed Sam." In his dressing gown and pyjamas, Dunne looked like any other young man having a weekend lie-in. Not like a policeman who'd forgotten to put his helmet on, the way the older coppers always looked off duty.

"Yeah, I know. I saw her go."

"Right," said Nigel, leading his guest through to the kitchen at the back. "Right, so you recognized her now. You never recognized her the other time, at Mr. Johnson's retirement do. She remembered you straight off, though. She was full of it on the way home—all about what a lad you used to be, all the things you and her brother got up to, in the good old days. You want coffee?"

"Thanks." Colin sat down at the pine table, while Nigel hooked two big, red mugs from a pine mug-tree on top of the

15

fridge. He looked around: nice place, clean, tidy, but homely. She kept a good house, Sam did. Always had done. Nigel moved around it with cautious pride, as if he couldn't quite believe his luck.

"How do you come to know her, then?"

"I know!" said Nigel, laughing, hovering over the boiling kettle. "The odd couple, eh? When I was at college, she worked in a pub there."

"Where?"

"Islington way. She did what you did, see—got out. Came north. She speaks very highly of you, you know, big fan of yours. More bottle than any man she's ever met, she reckons. You and her must have been pretty close, I suppose, in the old days."

"Mind if I smoke?" Nigel almost pulled a muscle in his haste to put a clean ashtray in front of Sergeant Mann. "Not that close. We saw each other around, got on all right." He lit up. "How'd you get on last night, then?"

"After you nicked my keys? Ah-ha! I know a few tricks, Skip. I don't know them all, like, not like you, not yet. But I know a few."

"Spare keys."

"I got a spare to just about every key in that station. Including the Super's drinks cabinet. I have, honest!"

He wouldn't have to kill both of them would he? Christ, yes, of course he would. He couldn't just kill the boy and leave the woman, a grieving not-quite-widow, with no pension and a big mouth. What a mess. He drank his coffee— nice coffee—smoked his cigarette, and thought, *Christ, what a mess.*

"I want to come in with you, Sarge. Please!"

"What?" Nigel was kneeling, actually fucking *kneeling,* on the linoleum by Colin's feet. "Get up, for God's sake."

"Sam reckons, the three of us, we could do real magic. Maybe I could get a job in the collator's office, maybe even at Area. It'd be great. Go on, Skip. It'd be like old times, only better."

The boy thought he was at it! The kid and the woman, they thought he was playing both sides. The hard man, the glamour boy, more bottle than anyone she'd ever met. They didn't know about his talent for disappearing; they thought it was all a great scam.

And Nigel wanted in. That was the blackmailer's price.

"They weren't *your* old days, Nigel. You don't know what you're talking about."

"Yeah, I know, Skip, but—"

Colin got up, walked towards the door. "Meet me in the Fat Duck, Monday night. Half six. We'll go for a ride."

"Thanks, Sarge! We going to do some business?"

"Yeah. That's fine."

"Thanks, Skip. Wait till Sam hears! I'll be ready, you'll see." His dressing gown swung open as he danced down the hall, to get the door open before Colin could reach it, and have to open it himself. "I'll be well ready, Skip, I promise you!"

Before leaving his flat on Monday evening, Colin stood in front of his hall mirror and gave himself a briefing. This is how it'll go:

18:30 hours—meet PC Dunne at the Fat Duck. Give him a good few drinks, let all the other coppers in the place remember how drunk he was when they left. *"I'd better give him a lift home, he's well gone."*

19:30 hours—leave the pub, drive to Nigel's place.

20:00 hours—arrive at Nigel's. Do her first—she looked stronger than the boy—then him.

17

20:20 to 20:35 hours—arrange the scene of crime.

20:40 hours—phone it in.

"When we got home, it was obvious she'd had a man there. She must have thought we'd be out all evening. We were planning to go on to a snooker club, but PC Dunne had too much to drink, so I had to take him home early. We arrived unexpectedly. Her attire was in disarray, she was dressed for bed, there was an empty wine bottle on the living room table. PC Dunne flew into a rage, shouting 'Oh no, not again, not again, you filthy slut, oh no not again.' He ran upstairs to the bedroom, then came down again, shouting 'In my bed, my own bloody bed, how could you, you slut, how could you.' I attempted to reason with him, but he was beyond it. 'I'll swing for you, you whoring cow,' he shouted, and, before I was able to intervene, he picked up a knife from the kitchen side, and drove it repeatedly into her chest and face. I wrestled with him, and managed to get him into an arm lock. Suddenly he went limp, and to my horror I realised that he was dead. I attempted emergency resuscitation on both victims, but without success. They were both dead. I can only surmise that the fatal injury to PC Dunne's neck occurred during my struggle with him. This is a nightmare that I will carry with me for the rest of my days. I do not require compassionate sick leave, as I believe that the best therapy for me would be to return to active duties as soon as possible."

It wasn't perfect, even for short notice. A lot of it would depend on Colin being a police officer, on Sergeant Colin Mann's own fine but not flashy record, working in his favour; on his version being accepted, without too much investigation.

But it was better than paying, especially when you don't even have the price that's being demanded.

No, it wasn't perfect, but it would have to do. He put on

his leather bomber, checked the pockets for fags, lighter, keys, wallet. Right then: better get it sorted.

The reluctant hero entered the pub at a minute before six o'clock, but saw no sign of the acolyte. Instead he saw, in his usual seat by the door, a sergeant from one of the other shifts sitting there puffing on that stupid, poncey pipe of his. Sherlock Holmes with a salt and pepper crew cut.

Colin approached Bob Miller with an affability that rarely exists, except between two men whose hatred is mutual, irrational and strong.

"Evening, Bob."

Miller reacted to Colin Mann's arrival with a deep and reptilian pleasure, even more so than a shared antipathy would normally demand. "You looking for your mate Dunne?"

"Yeah," said Colin, bunching his fists in his pockets. "You seen him?"

Miller shook his head from side to side, slowly, with his lips stretched wide, and his teeth together, clenching his poncey pipe, spreading the smoke in little bursts like a lawn sprinkler spreads water.

"No," he said. "Won't be seeing him either, not for a while. He's in custody."

"He's on duty? I thought he was—"

"No, he's not in the custody area, Colin," all drawled and sarky, so that it sounded like *custardy air-ear, Cor-lynne.* "He's *een custardy.* He's *beeeen* arrested. All right, mate?" Sergeant Miller turned back to his pint and his poncey pipe, pretending he thought the conversation was over.

"Right, fine," said Colin. For a moment he couldn't remember where he was. Or rather, he knew where he *was* of course, in the Fat Duck, but just for a second, no more than that, he couldn't quite think what was going on. "So what's he done then, Bob, he smacked someone, has he?" He tried to add a friendly laugh, but it came out like a nasal problem.

"Who, young Nigel?" Miller said, as if he'd forgotten who they were talking about. "No, nothing like that. Seems he's got some friends, wrong sort of friends, you know. They've been supplementing his private pension plan for him. For information received."

Fine, thought Colin. *Fine.*

"You want a drink?" said Miller.

"No, you're all right, Bob."

"Hope you haven't been getting too friendly with your little friend, Colin. Word is he's coughing his guts out in there. They start young these days, eh? Well, they've got the best teachers, haven't they?"

"Fine," said Colin. "That's fine, fine," and he began to walk out of the pub, unconsciously bumping a table here, jogging a drinker's elbow there, thinking to himself, *that's all right. That's fine. I done it once, I can do it again. Fine, that's fine.*

And as he got into the car (*Home first, grab some stuff? No, best not: straight for the motorway, that's better*), as he drove away from the Fat Duck, and from north London, and from being a copper (*Bristol? Yeah, Bristol's good, big city, plenty of opportunities for a man who'd been a crook and been a cop and knew which he preferred, but could do either*). As he left one life behind, and left behind the life behind that one, he was thinking, in some small department of his head, how glad he was that he hadn't, after all, had to kill anyone.

Not today, anyway.

Birmingham's bigger, of course. More people. No: rains all the time, can't stand the accent. Got a cousin lives in Birmingham. Bristol it is.

★ ★ ★ ★ ★

I'd been earning my living as a freelance writer and broadcaster for about four years before I made my first serious attempts at short story writing. I started with a series of science fiction stories (which are still unpublished as I write this); at that time I was more or less unaware that there existed a market for short crime fiction.

In 1992 or 1993 I began reviewing crime novels, and became an associate member of the Crime Writers' Association. At about the same time I discovered *Hardboiled*, a marvellous magazine published in New York by Gary Lovisi. I underwent a moment of self-discovery which will be familiar to many writers: "Hello," I thought. "I could do that."

I wrote three stories: "The Set-Up Man" (which appears in this collection), "The Hampstead Vegetable Heist" (which doesn't appear here, for reasons of space; it sold to the CWA's 1994 anthology, *3rd Culprit*, and was later broadcast on BBC Radio 4), and "History Repeats. . . ."

The title and first line of this story arrived in my mind unsought, and all I had to do was write them down and carry on from there. These days, I tend to labour long and hard on my short stories. Writing, like most things in life, becomes harder with practice. Maxim Jakubowski, Britain's leading anthologist—who I am sure had never previously heard of me—bought it for *Constable New Crimes 2*. It was short listed for the CWA's short story Dagger Award, in the inaugural year of that prize, and was reprinted twice within a year—once in the UK, once in the US.

Subsequent events proved that I was experiencing that phenomenon known as beginner's luck; things have never gone quite so smoothly for me since. Still, what I say is—better to have beginner's luck, than no luck at all.

NO NIGHT BY MYSELF

"I've got to go into hospital straight after Christmas."

"Shit," says Diplomacy. "Sorry to hear that, mate."

"Yeah. Royal Free, second day after Boxing Day. For tests."

"I'm really sorry to hear that, mate."

"Mind you," I say. "Tests—they're test-mad these days, aren't they? I mean, you go to the doc with a mouth ulcer these days, they send you down the hospital for tests."

"That's true," says Diplomacy, sipping the top off his pint. "There again, my brother-in-law had a mouth ulcer, wouldn't clear up, they sent him down the Free for tests, and we buried him six months later."

What's so funny about that is, the actual reason they call him Diplomacy is because he used to be a chauffeur for some foreign bloke, some Arab who lived on Ambassadors' Row. That's what's so funny about that.

"And I'll tell you what," says Diplomacy. "He must've been a good ten years younger than you, my brother-in-law. Mid-thirties, he was."

"Well, anyway," I say. "I haven't got a mouth ulcer."

"So what you doing for Christmas, Madness?" he says. "Usual is it, going over your gran's, as per?"

I shake my head. Not like *no;* more like *slightly annoyed.* "Gran died, yeah? In the summer."

"Oh Christ," says Diplomacy. "Sorry mate, of course. I

hadn't really forgotten, you did tell me, I just wasn't thinking. Sorry, mate. June, wasn't it? Only I remember, because Wimbledon was on, Cherry watches it on the telly. So what you got lined up, then? Hotel room full of teenage nymphos, yeah?"

"I don't know," I say. "Nothing, really."

Diplomacy wipes his hand across his mouth, picks up his lager and finishes it. Right down the hatch, fast as you like. He stands up to go. "Well, whatever you do, I hope you have a good one, mate. Look, I got to be going. Wife, etc. Christmas Eve, you know—last minute instructions and what-have-you." He claps a hand on my shoulder, picks up his lighter and some small change off the counter. "Be seeing you, Madness. Have fun, yeah? And don't get caught!"

And he's gone.

So has almost everybody by now, it's getting late. Few faces I half know over the other side of the bar, younger than me, they're getting ready to go, too. Buying bottles to take out.

I call over to them, "Having a party, lads?"

They make out they haven't heard me. If they are having a party, it's not one I'm invited to.

There's never been a Christmas in my life I didn't spend with my gran. I've been inside a few times, yeah, but even then, as it happened, I was never inside at Christmas. Always at my gran's.

The boys go off to their party or whatever, and it's just me and the barman. He sees me still sitting there, and brings over a parcel; a heavy cardboard box tied up with string.

"Jim said to give you this," he says, putting it on the counter. I pick it up and put it down by my feet.

"Oh yeah, cheers, son. I was expecting it."

"Right," says the barman, polishing the counter, collecting empty glasses.

23

"Jim say anything about it, did he?"

"No," he says, "only that you'd know what it was about."

"Yeah, that's all right," I say. "I know about it."

"Which I don't," says the barman. "Okay? I don't know anything about it."

I finish my drink, and I'm about to see what the chances are of getting another, when the barman takes the glass from me and says, "Right, cheers then, Madness. Mind how you go."

He's in a rush. Not working tomorrow, wants to get over his girlfriend's for Christmas.

"Yeah, fair enough, mate," I say. "Let me get a couple of bottles to take out, right?"

"No problem," says the barman. "What's your pleasure?"

A couple of bottles—Jesus. I have *never* spent Christmas on my own, not ever. Never alone.

I'm walking through Golders Green, walking home to my room, thinking maybe there'll be a message on the board by the pay phone in the entrance hall—"So-and-so rang while you were out, can you come for X-mas dinner?"—but really, I can't think of anyone who might leave a message like that. If there is anyone, I've already rung them.

And all the time I'm walking, my mind keeps going: *Never alone, never alone, never alone.*

The parcel the barman gave me is awkward to carry, and the bag with the bottles in it is clanking against my leg, so I stop for a moment, put everything down, light a fag.

I'm stretching my arms, and I look round, and I'm standing right outside this really nice house. I've walked down this road thousands of times, and it is a nice road, all the houses look like quality. Detached, big garage to the side, an in-and-out gravel drive, with a rose bush or something in a brown earth island in the middle of a tiny front lawn. The windows have that lead stuff on them, like old-fashioned houses, but they're not, they're younger than me, these houses. I remember when they went up.

They always look nice, but tonight, Christmas Eve, this particular house looks *really* nice. They've got a holly wreath on the door, with a bright red bow on it, and I can see all lights through the windows, and a paper-chain. So I pick up Jim's parcel, and the bag of booze, and scrunch my way up the drive and knock on the door. I have to use my knuckles, because the actual knocker is covered by the holly.

It's gone midnight now, and I'm thinking maybe it's too late, maybe I shouldn't be knocking so late at night; everyone might be in bed. But almost immediately, the door opens, opens wide and welcome, and I walk in.

"Hello?" says the woman who's opened the door. Pleasant-looking woman, very white cheeks with red dots on them and light, thin hair. Just a few years younger than me, I reckon. Wearing a dress, quite smart, and some tiny pearls round her neck.

"*Excuse* me," she says, still holding the front door open. Then she forgets the door, and calls out: "Tony!"

Meanwhile, I'm opening a door off the hall, on the left, peering into a room which at first I think, from the smell of it, is empty, unused. A spare room downstairs—well, when you've got this many rooms, why not? No point heating them all up just for the sake of using them. But when I turn the light on, I see a big, green-topped desk, with a computer screen on it, and there's a swivel chair and a filing cabinet, and that. Like an office at home. In case you get snowed in or something, I suppose.

"Excuse me?"

I look round. There's a man standing there, late thirties,

bald at the front, wearing suit trousers and a striped, ironed shirt, but without the jacket, and no tie. I switch the light off in the spare office, close the door behind me, and slip past the man—not pushing, not roughly—because I've just caught sight of the living room, across the hall.

The man, the husband obviously, pinches at my sleeve as I walk into the big room—light's already on in here—and says: "I *said*, excuse me! Do I know you? Can I help you?" The wife's standing behind him, the red spots on her cheeks getting bigger.

Beautiful room. Very good quality furniture, wallpaper, all that. Very warm, from an artificial coal fire at the far end. Really nice room. These people have got taste, not just money. Little framed pictures on the walls, of country scenes. No telly—they probably keep that in another room, a special TV room—but a huge Christmas tree, in the corner behind the door, absolutely covered with flickering lights, and tinsel, and presents wrapped up in shiny paper that reflects the room. One of the biggest and best trees I've ever seen. Mind, in my opinion they ought to put it in the window, not hidden away behind the door. Make the place more inviting from outside. I might mention that to the woman, if it doesn't seem rude.

"Look," says the man, trying to stand in front of me, trying to bar my way as I start moving along the hall towards the back of the house. "Now look here, I don't know who you are, but unless you have some reason for being here I must insist you leave immediately." And he points towards the front door, which is letting in quite a draft.

It's the kitchen I want now, so I duck under the man's arm—he's shorter than me, but I'm quicker than him—and as I head down the long hall, I hear him behind me, saying: "It's all right, Sarah, you just stay there."

Before you get to the actual kitchen at Sarah and Tony's, you have to pass through the dining room. This is also beautifully laid out, with a pretty red tablecloth over a big round table—it'd seat six, easily—and there's decorations round the room and on the table itself, and Christmas crackers by each tablemat.

But I'm concentrating on the kitchen for the moment, so I walk straight through. The man's been following me, sort of snapping round my heels from room to room, and I haven't been paying much attention. Suddenly, now, I find his arm is around my neck and he's trying to steer me out of the back door, the door from the kitchen into the garden.

Too bloody cold for that, thank you, so I push him down onto a stool—it's a big kitchen, you hardly need a dining room with a kitchen this size—and he falls off the stool and bumps him bum on the floor. His wife, standing in the archway that leads back into the dining room, gasps, and cries out: "Oh my God, what do you want from us? It's Christmas, for God's sake!"

Funny thing is, I thought they didn't have Christmas, this lot. I don't know, maybe that's the Muslims, or whatever. So I look at them now, the man getting up off the floor, slowly, trying to get the stool between him and me, and the woman standing in the archway, arms crossed tight, shaking a bit. I look at them. Or, let *them* have a look at me, really. I've already seen them, corner-of-the-eyes stuff, now they can see me.

Now I'll listen to them. It's not that I haven't been hearing them before, all their questions, it's just that I've been busy. Had to have a good look around, see if this is the sort of home I thought it was. Like, have they done the place up nice? Got all the right grub in? Put up decent decorations etc, like my gran would. I mean, not everybody bothers these days; I don't want to stay if they're not going to do it properly.

So I look at the man, look back at the woman, and now she's got a little boy with her. Behind her, don't know if she's seen him yet; I never heard him come in. About ten years old, just standing there, wondering what's going on. Pyjamas, dressing gown, Fred Flintstone slippers.

"Hello, son," I say.

They both swing round, look at the boy. The man says, "Oh God," and the woman grabs the boy, holds him close.

We walk back into the dining room. Well, I walk in, they follow me. I'll tell you what, people say they're mean, don't they? Jews and that. But not this lot—I can tell that by the Christmas crackers. I've never seen crackers like them! Much bigger than the ones you normally see, much fatter, and the paper looks really classy, dead expensive. Still, people come out with a lot of prejudices, and they're not always accurate in my experience.

I put the parcel the barman gave me, and the bag of booze, on a small table by the window. I unwrap the parcel, using my penknife to cut through the string. I don't bother saving the paper, because it's not that sort of paper. Just ordinary brown paper, I screw it up and chuck it in a little wastepaper basket under the table. I take the gun out of the parcel, and put it on the table next to the carrier bag.

So then I turn round, look at them, give them a big smile.

"Hello," I say. "Happy Christmas."

"What do you want?" says the man. "Just tell us what you want."

"I've come to stay," I tell him. "I've come to stay for Christmas. Look," I say, "I've brought this." And I pull the bottles out of the bag. A big bottle of scotch—malt whisky, for Christmas—and one of ginger wine. Seasonal fare. I hold them out to the woman, and after a moment she comes over and takes them.

"Thank you," she says, very soft, staring at me as she backs away.

"That's right, love," I says. "Just put them with the rest, eh?"

The boy's sitting on one of the chairs at the dining table. He'd better not mess up the place settings, they been done beautifully. The man watches his wife take the booze, my festive gifts, over to a handsome sideboard behind the table, where there's bottles of every kind of booze you can imagine lined up in rows, glinting in the jolly light.

"Oh my God," says the man, so quiet I can hardly hear him. "Oh my God, he's mad."

Now the funny thing about that is, the only reason they call me Madness, down the pub, is because I used to really like that pop group—the one that was called "Madness." That's what's so funny about that.

The man looks at the gun, the pistol, sitting on the table. "Just tell us what you want," he says again. "We don't even know who you are, I swear we don't!"

So I pick up the gun, and point it at the boy a bit. My finger's nowhere near the trigger, there's no danger. It's not mine, the gun, I haven't used one of these since I was a kid. It belongs to a big noise called Jim, only he's made a date with some pal on the robbery squad to raid his house on Boxing Day, so could I look after it for a couple of days (which obviously I can, no-one's going to raid my bedsit, are they?), and he'll owe me a good drink, mate. *After* Christmas, naturally, when things have quieted down.

I smile at the man, smile at the woman. The boy looks a bit scared. In fact, I'm a bit worried about the boy. I mean, I haven't got anything for him—the booze is okay for his mum and dad, but I never thought to bring anything for a kid. It was all a bit spur of the moment, if you know what I mean. Never mind—I've had a good idea. Yeah, he'll love that, that'll do nicely.

Meanwhile: manners, Madness, please! Introductions first.

"I'm your cousin," I tell them. "I'm your cousin Madness, and I've come to stay for Christmas, I've come to surprise you for a lovely family Christmas. Happy Christmas," I say.

No response from the husband, but the wife—she's looking at the gun pointing at the boy—she walks over towards me, so she's standing between the gun and the kid, clever girl, and she says: "Happy Christmas." She swallows, there's a little tear there I think, then she says it again, louder: "Happy Christmas. I'm Sarah, and my son's name is Daniel."

"Happy Christmas, Daniel," I says, giving him a grin.

He doesn't look at his mum or his dad, he looks straight at me and says, "Happy Christmas, Cousin Madness."

I say Happy Christmas again, and laugh. We'll all have a laugh about that, later on, the way he says it with that straight face, like he thinks maybe I really *am* his cousin, only nobody's ever thought to mention me before! Good manners, that's what that is. Good, decent, family upbringing. "Good boy," I say.

Sarah looks over at her husband, sort of nudges him with her eyes, and says, "And this is my husband, Tony."

"Happy Christmas, Tony," I say.

He looks at his wife, looks at me, takes off his glasses and wipes his face with his shirt cuff. "Happy Christmas," he says.

He's got his hands underneath his armpits now, squeezing them, so I don't go to shake hands with him. Wouldn't be right, I don't want to embarrass him.

I put the gun in my belt. There; that's the formal part over with.

We're in the living room, the room with the beautiful tree in it, having a nice Christmas Eve drink. Wine, in fact; they've opened a bottle specially, which is only what you'd expect from this sort of person. People of this quality, they're never thrown by unexpected guests. Nice drop of wine, as it goes, not my usual tipple, but it's going down very pleasantly.

I feel good. Sitting here, enjoying the lights from the tree, curtains drawn, fire up, all cosy. Christmassy. Wondering about the presents under the tree although, obviously, I know none of them can be for me. They weren't expecting me, that'd be asking too much, but even so, it's fun to wonder. That parcel there—is that a book? A record? That great big one, what's that: a bike for the lad? A new toolkit for Dad?

Which reminds me: presents. "I hope you like the scotch, Tony? I see you're a wine drinker, if I'd known, obviously . . ."

"No, no, that's . . . that's fine," says Tony. "Isn't it, dear? That's, yes, that's lovely."

"Lovely," says Sarah. "Very thoughtful."

"It's a good one," I say, not boasting, but, you know—it *is* a good one.

"Yes," says Tony. "No that's, really, that's fine. My favourite."

"I am glad," I say. "We'll have a drop later, eh?"

Daniel's in bed. As he should be, of course, nearly one o'clock Christmas morning. Dreaming about his presents.

"Thing is," I say, a bit embarrassed, even though it's hardly my fault. "The boy—I just didn't think."

"Doesn't matter!" they both say at once. I've still got the

gun in my belt, obviously, but to be honest, what I always think is, after the first few minutes—whatever situation you're in—a weapon doesn't really make much difference. Things are either calm or they're not, and if they're not a weapon's just going to make things worse, right? Tonight, I rather wish I'd left it in the bag. Didn't really need it, not really, and there's always a risk it'll cause an atmosphere.

"No, well," I say, "maybe, but I've had an idea anyway." I reach into my pocket, bring out the knife, and chuck it over to Tony. He flinches: butter fingers.

"It's not new, obviously," I say. "But it's in good nick, I've kept it nice. And it's a good knife, cost me a few bob. I was thinking, you know, perhaps Sarah could just wrap it up, bung it under the tree with the rest. I mean, I know it's second-hand, but I think he'll like it. Every boy likes a knife, right?" And then I look at Tony seriously, because it's his house, after all, his son. "Unless, you know, if you don't think it's suitable. I mean, if you think he's too young or whatever?"

But no problem there, they're fine about it, thank me for the knife, Sarah says she'll wrap it, she's sure Daniel'll be delighted. So that's good. Anyway, it's getting late now, I'm feeling a bit knackered. Been mixing my drinks today, that's the truth, which is always a bad move!

"Well, all good things must come to an end," I say, and I stand up, stretch my arms over my head.

Sarah and Tony leap up like they've been bit by a dog. "Wait!" says Tony.

"Bedtime," I tell him.

They look at each other. "Oh my God . . ." says Tony, sinking back into the chair.

"Right," says the wife. "Fine. Well—Madness. Why don't you help yourself? Any room, they're all aired. And there's towels in the bathroom cupboard." She looks down at her husband, then back at me. "I think—Tony and I, we'll probably stay up for a bit, see if there's a film on or something."

I give her a smile. "I think we should all turn in, don't you? Late nights make cross mornings, that's what my old gran always said."

So we all turn in. Just as well: don't want to be grouchy, Christmas morning.

About an hour and a half later, Sarah falls right over me, bang! Straight on the deck.

Not her fault—I'm lying on the carpet right outside their room, jacket for a pillow, gun in my hand.

She's got her dressing gown on, and shoes. Outdoor shoes. And a torch. I help her to her feet, nothing broken, and we look at each other for a while. Slightly awkward moment, all round.

She looks at the gun, can't help herself, then looks at me. "Are you angry with me?"

As if! I mean, come on, it's her family isn't it? She's got to have a go, right, got to keep trying, else how would she live with herself if anything happened? Fair enough, hell, I understand all that. But then that's her, see: thinking of me, has she upset me, not thinking of herself. Smashing lady, Sarah.

"I hope your Tony knows what a lucky bloke he is," I say, but she pulls her dressing gown round her more tightly and I think maybe she's got the wrong idea. So I take a step away from her, lean against the banister, light a ciggie, very casual.

"I usually go to my gran's," I tell her.

She nods. I offer her a cigarette—better late than never, Mr. Manners!—and she takes it, lets me light it, though it's obvious she's not a smoker. "Did your gran die?" she asks.

33

See what I mean? Thinks of others, notices things, works it out. Sympathetic.

But this is Christmas, and I've imposed enough already. I wouldn't actually mind crying on her shoulder, I'm not ashamed to say it, but it's not actually mine to cry on is it? So I sniff, pretend a yawn, and say: "Well, better get some sleep, yeah? Big day tomorrow!"

I wake in the morning rested and relaxed. Kipping on floors doesn't bother me, slept on more floors than beds, me. Anyway: it's Christmas morning! And there's that special feeling, I don't care how old you are, it never goes away does it? The time ever comes when you don't feel that special excitement of Christmas morning—I don't care if you're nine or ninety-nine—then, son, you are ready for the grave!

Well let me tell you, no danger of Christmas morning not being special here, in this beautiful house, with these fine, kind people. It's like a dream! I wish my gran could've been here, she'd have loved it.

Great big breakfast, all the family together. Lovely grub. Nothing heavy, got to leave room for later, but very satisfactory. They both get the meal, Sarah and Tony, which is nice. Lady like that, she deserves a considerate husband, and I'm pleased to see she's got one. Because it can be a chore for the women, Christmas Day, if the men don't help out. So I volunteer for the washing-up, least I can do.

While I'm doing that, I take the gun out of my belt, slip it in my inside jacket pocket and hang the jacket behind the kitchen door. I feel better for that: guns and Christmas, you know, doesn't seem right, does it? Daniel sees me doing it—impatient to open his presents, he's come into the kitchen to find out what's keeping me—so I tell him he's not to touch my jacket, OK? And of course he says OK, good lad.

Opening the presents makes me a bit sad just for a while.

Nothing for me, naturally, and that makes me think of Christmas at my gran's. She always got me a nice jumper, a record, whatever. Still, I cheer up when Daniel's so pleased with my knife. I don't think he's just being polite, I think he's really pleased. Well, it is a good knife, even if it is second-hand.

Before you know it, it's almost lunchtime. We pull lots of crackers, especially me and Daniel—two daft kids!—and bloody good crackers they are, just as I thought. Really good gifts, things you can actually use, not plastic crap, and a big bang, and classy hats. But the jokes are still crap. "What do you call an octopus with seven legs? A seven-legged octopus." I don't think that's funny. I mean I *get* it, I just don't think it's funny. You pay this sort of money you should get a decent joke. Still, never mind. Minor point.

Daniel's allowed to put the telly on now, sits there in front of it playing with all his new stuff, as us grown-ups enjoy a little sherry while the meal finishes cooking in the oven.

Sarah coughs, clears her throat, and says, "Well, a Merry Christmas to you, Madness, and a Happy New Year." She's looking more relaxed now, glad to have all the preparations over, I suppose.

"Actually, it's been a jolly bad year for me," I say. Well, why not? I'm amongst friends, don't have to be shy. Say what I'm feeling. "A jolly bad year all round. I'll be glad to see the back of it. Or at least, I would be if I didn't know that the next one will be just as bad, or worse."

"I'm sorry to hear that," she says. "Why has it been such a bad year, if you don't mind me asking?"

"Not at all," I say. "Kind of you to ask." But I don't really know what to say now. Don't want to tell them about the hospital, all that, don't want to put the mockers on. Ruin their Christmas with someone else's bad luck. So I say: "Oh just this and that, you know." I put a finger in my mouth, waggle a tooth about. "Bad teeth, for one thing. Feels like they're all about to fall out. Keeps me awake, sometimes." Funny thing is, that's not a lie, I have had a lot of trouble with my teeth just lately.

"Have you," says Tony, "I mean, have you seen a dentist? I suppose you must have."

"No, I don't like dentists."

"My wife's brother's a dentist," he says.

Whoops. "No, no offence, I'm not prejudiced or anything," I tell her. "I'm sure your brother's a very good dentist, they can't all be crooks, can they? Anyway, I'm sure it wasn't your brother I saw last time."

"No," she says.

"Unless—he's not an Australian bloke, is he? Finchley Road?"

"No," she says.

"Red hair, big ears?"

"No, that's not him."

"Well," says Tony, "no, not Finchley Road. He's bald. He has got big ears, though." His wife gives him a look, and he shuts up.

It's nice in here. Warm, cheerful, few friends having a drink, rattling their jaws, chatting about their little troubles. A thought strikes me.

"What you two doing for New Year's, then?"

She gurgles, just for a second, very quietly. He opens his mouth preparatory for a quick stutter, but she puts her hand on his arm, says: "Well, you know, Madness, we, sort of, we don't in fact celebrate the same New Year. We're Jewish, remember."

Embarrassing! "Oh right," I say. "Sorry, no offence."

"None taken," she says, very gracious. "I hope you'll have

a very happy one, anyway."

"Oh, sure," I say. "Well, never mind, New Year's different, eh? Pubs are open, last train on the Tube's free. Go anywhere, New Year. Many options, several choices. Yeah, don't worry, won't be on my own New Year."

"You don't like to be on your own, Madness?" she says.

Very perceptive, that seems to me. A very unselfish lady, very open to thoughts about others. "Well," I say, playing it down, like it's no big thing. "It's just that, you know, I mean, you don't come into this world alone, do you? Your mum's there, and the nurse and that, and you don't go out of it alone, do you?"

"You don't?" says Tony.

"Actually, no," I say. "This bloke gets in the pub, he used to work in a crematorium, and he says they shove you through twelve at a time, saves on the fuel."

Bloody nice thing to talk about on Christmas Day! *Idiot*. I try to think of some way to make a joke of it, without making it worse, when there's a knock on the door, and my hosts freeze, staring at each other.

Christ, now that *is* embarrassing. They were expecting company! And I never thought to ask, and they were too polite to mention it. But now I think, yeah, six places set in the dining room. Hell's bells.

The really embarrassing thing, of course, is that there's nothing I can do about it, not given the circumstances. We're just going to have to hope the visitors go away, and then we'll really have to get our heads together trying to come up with some excuse for later, for why Sarah and Tony didn't answer the door. And that's not going to be easy.

They do go away, but not quickly and not for very long. The phone rings all through lunch (great lunch, even if we are all a little distracted), and then just as we're settling down in front of the box again, the visitors return. Well they would, wouldn't they, when you think about it? I mean, they certainly know they haven't got the wrong day! And if we don't answer this time, chances are they'll get worried, call the cops.

"Right," I say, positioning myself in the living room doorway. "Look, I'm sorry about this, but this is what we're going to have to do. Daniel?" He looks up from the telly. "Lend me your new knife a moment, will you? And come and stand over here with me." Because I don't fancy nipping to the kitchen to fetch the gun; the people outside might see me through the hall window. "Sarah, you stay there behind me. Tony, you go to the door, tell them they can't come in, you've got a contagious disease."

"Contagious disease?" says Tony, almost laughing at the idea. He wants to take things more seriously, that bloke, no criticism intended, but he does. I know it's not a great plan, but it might send them away for a few minutes at least, long enough for me to fetch my jacket, dash off out the back. No time for good manners now, unfortunately.

"Go on, love," says Sarah. "Tell them measles, we've all got measles, and could they come back later when we might be feeling better." Good girl!

"And, Tony?" I say. "Don't mumble, please." Daniel's standing right in front of me, I've got one hand on his shoulder, and the knife in my other hand. Obviously, I don't want to scare the boy, but Tony gets the message.

I keep out of sight, but I can hear him. "Measles . . . blah blah . . . not to worry . . . blah blah . . . give us a ring later, Jeremy . . . blah blah . . ."

It's worked. Won't work for long, I'll have to get out soonish, and carefully too, but at least there's been no need for any of the sort of unpleasantness which could have ruined

Christmas for everyone.

The door shuts, I look round at the family—like, *Phew!* Like, relax folks, panic over, back to the festivities. Only, I look at Sarah, and she's got that damn gun of Jim's—wish I'd never seen the damn thing, I really do—pointing right at me. Steady as you like, two-handed grip like the cops on telly, pointing right at the bridge of my nose. Well, fair enough, I didn't tell Daniel "Don't mention it to anyone," I just told him "Don't touch it." It's not like he's disobeyed me.

I look at Sarah's eyes. Red flush from chest to cheeks, very angry. The funny thing is, I don't think she's going to shoot me. I'm not an expert on people or anything, but I've looked at a lot of faces in my time, and I don't think she'll shoot me. What I think she'll do is, I think she'll lock the gun up in a cupboard upstairs, not showing me where it is, then I think she'll go outside and throw the key down a drain, and then she'll say, like, "Right, let's all go back in and finish our cheese and nuts, and then I think you owe everybody an apology, Madness, don't you?" Maybe she'll even laugh and say, "Get my brother round to look at your teeth, shall we?"

I don't know for sure, obviously, I'm not a mind-reader, but I *think* that's what she'll do. That's what my gran would have done, anyway.

★ ★ ★ ★ ★

I wrote this around Christmastime 1994, and it first appeared in the 1995 Bouchercon anthology, *No Alibi*. It's been a good little worker for me over the years, attracting one or two reprint fees and some positive attention, but still I'm not entirely happy with it.

As a young, single man in the early 1980s, I spent several extremely enjoyable Christmases which centred on the pubs of north London. It was that feeling that I set out to recapture when I began this story—in other words, it was intended to be a warm, nostalgic, even cosy piece. Instead, I ended up with this grim tale. I'm sure I'm not the only writer who has discovered that the type of material I'm *good* at writing is not necessarily the same type that I most *want* to write; and, of course, it's axiomatically easier to write nasty than it is to write nice. That's one reason why P. G. Wodehouse is so revered—and so unrivalled.

THE SET-UP MAN

"The point is," I said, "I'm not a detective."

"The point is," said Alias The Fish, "you owe me a favour. That's the point."

As far as I knew, I didn't owe him anything. But I think the way you get to owe John McNeil a favour is that one day you're standing in the pub, a few places down the bar from him, laughing and joking with your mates, and the noise you're making begins to irritate him, and he looks over at you with that frozen contempt that never leaves his skeletal face, and decides to kill you, for some peace and quiet. And then he decides that he can't be bothered, and that he'll have another drink and tell you to shut up instead. And then because he hasn't killed you, as far as he's concerned you owe him a favour. I think that's how it works. Anyway, was I going to argue?

"Yeah, well, Mr. McNeil—"

"You can call me Alias The," he said, and he almost smiled, the way a dead fish might almost smile if it wasn't really very amused and was just being polite. Shit! Could a man that evil have a sense of humour?

"Yeah, well, Mr. McNeil, obviously it's a favour I'd be more than happy to pay back anyplace anytime anywhere, but I'm not a detective, see, I'm a freelance researcher. I think you need a detective. See, a researcher, that's not really the same thing."

In the Three Crowns, the pub I usually drink in, and the pub John McNeil occasionally graces with his patronage, he's known as Alias The Fish. Seems some time ago he got his name in the papers (he was acquitted, of course), and that name was "John McNeil, alias The Fish." I never heard anyone call him The Fish—I mean, who'd dare?—but Alias The Fish has that sort of ironic, north London twist to it, and he doesn't seem to mind.

Far as I can tell it's one of the few things he doesn't mind. McNeil doesn't smoke, except a cigar on Christmas Day. He always wears a tie. He never swears—"Never uses language," as his fat, stupid, fur-coated wife likes to boast, like that makes him some kind of gentleman—and he never drinks anything but one or two gin and tonics. He's quite tall, and sits with his back perfectly straight. He's in the construction business, whatever that means. Well actually, I think I know what it means in his case.

People in the pub like having him around. A real villain. Makes all the would-be gangsters and the petty thieves feel like they're close to royalty. Camden Town's full of people who think they're villains, but Alias T. Fish ain't the sort of bloke who goes around *thinking* he's something. He's the sort of bloke who goes around telling innocent bystanders like me to find the man who'd run over his granddaughter's dog, so that he could have him hurt.

I'd never met his granddaughter, but I could just picture her: fat and stupid and fur-coated like her granny. But younger.

Now, I like dogs. Always liked dogs. Had one when I was a kid, in fact, even though we lived on the third floor. Someone runs a dog over, leaves it to die, doesn't even bother to stop— I think that's dreadful, shouldn't be allowed. If it was my dog got run over, I'd want to punch the bastard driver right in the mouth. Or better yet, in the balls.

But that's one thing. What Alias The Fish was talking about was something nastier. Finding the culprit, weeks after the event, and paying or perhaps just plain ordering two guys to hold him down while another guy goes over him, silently, systematically breaking every bone he owns and leaving him very hurt but not entirely dead. That's cold, vicious.

On the other hand . . . rather the dog-squasher than me.

"I'm not a detective," I said, for maybe the three hundredth time, sitting in that ugly, hot, stinking cafe in Camden, the sort of place you wouldn't expect my new pal Alias The to be seen dead in. Which worried me. "I don't know anything about finding people."

"You don't have to find him, young man. I know who he is, I know where he lives. He worked for me. Name's Hughes. Since he killed the dog, he's gone to ground. All you've got to do is bring him to a meet. Somewhere nice and quiet."

McNeil finished his tea. "You're my set-up man."

You ever wonder who votes Conservative? This is who. He lives in the suburbs, plays golf, probably a churchgoer, and I was betting his granddaughter'd get a pony to take her mind off the dead dog.

I phoned my mate Bobby—I knew where he'd be, in the boozer. Like most of my friends, Bobby has been unemployed so long he doesn't even know he's unemployed any more. He thinks what he's got is a life. "It's Stan," I said. I didn't need to give a surname. I must be the only Stan in the whole of Britain under the age of about fifty-three.

"Yeah, I know Hughes. They call him Little Gitface."

"Why?" I asked.

"I dunno. Because he is one, I suppose."

"I need to see him urgently. Could you get him to meet

me? Tonight, if possible. There's a drink in it for you." I gave Bobby the place and the time.

"Yeah, no problem. Someone paying you for this?"

I laughed. "I doubt it."

Matter of fact, that was the least of my problems. I was still living off a research job I'd done a couple of weeks previously. A TV company was doing a piece on London's only growth industry—hostels for the homeless. A great racket. You buy a derelict bed and breakfast place, fill it up with desperate people, like worms in a bait-tin, and the social security pays you whatever rent you care to ask for. I'd done the ground-work, and scored five hundred quid for it. For the first time in a long time I was solvent—that is, if you count a whole life-time as being a long time.

That night, on my way to the meet, outside the Tube sta-tion, a man dressed in a suit that looked as if someone had been buried in it several years ago—a man who looked as if he was the one who'd been buried—asked me if I had any spare change. I reached into my pocket, found a one-pound coin. I have this simple rule, call it the Code of the Stans. Any time the cash I got on me is more than the price of a beer and a packet of cigarettes, I give a little to the beggars. *There but for the grace of being able to read and write and talk outta the side of my mouth go I,* is what I always think.

As I lay the coin in the upturned claw of the disinterred man, the wind changed direction and I almost threw up. If I live till next October I'll still only be twenty-six, but even I'm old enough to remember when Underground stations didn't stink of piss all day long. Those lucky people on the Moscow Metro. They don't know what they've got to look forward to.

The tramp must have seen my nose wrinkling. "Yeah," he said, like one commuter to another, "disgusting, innit?

Course, this used to be a real nice area. Then all the col-
oureds moved in." I took the coin back, told the undead man
I hoped he'd die soon, and walked on. The Code of the Stans
says: if you're rich enough to worry about immigrants low-
ering the tone of the neighbourhood, then you certainly don't
need my handouts.

Somewhere quiet, McNeil had said. This was quiet. Pretty
dark, not overlooked by any windows, not on the way to anywhere. A little alley behind some fast food places that hadn't
been fast enough to beat the recession. Empty. Very quiet.

Its only landmark was a phone booth—cleverly positioned
by the phone company so as to be of minimum use to anybody—which I checked as soon as I arrived. It was working. So
I could call Alias The Fish, waiting in his car around the
corner, let him know when Gitface got here. Great.

I still didn't know what I was going to do. Warn Gitface,
and get myself killed? No, I don't think so. Give him a couple
of thumps on my own account, and tell McNeil the job was
done? Maybe. Maybe he just wouldn't turn up. That'd be
good. That'd be favourite.

It was quiet, all right. All I could hear was my heart
shouting "Lemme outta this chest!" and a small, annoying
drilling noise somewhere at the back of my brain.

I checked my watch. Five to ten. Just time for a quick
phone call.

"Bobby, listen, this Gitface character. Describe him a bit
more, will you?" He did. I still couldn't pin the memory
down. I meet a lot of people all the time. But I knew that little
shit Bobby was describing. Knew him from somewhere.
"What kind of car does he drive?"

"You kidding? Look, this bloke lives in some crappy room,
like, one step up from Cardboard City, yeah? He don't own a

car same reason you don't own a yacht. What's this all about anyway, Stan?"

"It's a long story, mate, and a silly one. I'll tell you some time. Basically, it's to do with John McNeil's granddaughter's dog getting run over."

The telephone couldn't make up its mind whether to transmit an incredulous silence or a derisive laugh. It tried both at once.

"Not only hasn't John's granddaughter got a dog," barked Bobby, "but John hasn't even got a fucking granddaughter!"

I would have asked him to enlarge on that interesting news, but I had to hang up. Because just then, into the alley, came Little Gitface. And one pace behind him, there was John McNeil, Alias The Fish, alongside a great big giant of a murderous-looking bastard, who was obviously employed by John in some capacity, and probably not as a secretary-receptionist.

"Hey, Mr. McNeil," I called, steering my cotton-wool legs out of the phone booth. "I see you and your pal met up all right." He didn't answer, just kept on strolling towards me, casual as a landslide, his assistant right beside him, while Gitface scampered ahead, like a house-trained mongrel.

"That's him all right, Mr. McNeil," the little man said, a spittle-streaked sneer on his face to show how pleased he was feeling with himself. And then I recognized him, knew where I'd seen him before, just before he said, "That's the boy been round your bed and breakfast, spyin' and tape-recordin' and pokin' his nose in."

Alias The Fish looked at me, not at the little man, as he quietly asked him, "You definite?"

"Definite, Mr. McNeil. Definite." Gitface stretched out an excited hand, so one long finger was almost touching my chest. "That's him."

✪

As a reader, I followed what I now know to have been a typical path into crime fiction. When I was a young child I read comics and Enid Blyton, and between the ages of about ten and twelve I must have read almost everything by Agatha Christie, chiefly for the sake of her puzzles. In my teens, I read Raymond Chandler for the sake of his language. I then defected to science fiction, almost entirely, until one day during my mid-twenties my girlfriend urged me to read a Ruth Rendell book. And that was it; I was now, and for the first time knew myself to be, a crime fiction fan.

Some people consider genre labelling restrictive, but I'm all for it—I like to know what I'm getting, before I get it. At my local public library in those days, the labelling was actual: the spines of crime novels had *CRI* stamped on them. I began sampling at random, and soon discovered a type of American writing that greatly appealed to me: stories told mostly in dialogue, with lots of dark humour and colourful characters.

"The Set-Up Man" was the first crime story I ever wrote, and the first I ever sold (to *Hardboiled* magazine). Some years later, a sequel to this story appeared on the *Blue Murder* e-zine.

THE SHORTEST DISTANCE

Ugly people rule the world. All that frustrated sexual energy has to go somewhere.

My new client, Noel Bell, was certainly ugly, and he definitely ruled the world. His large, pink head had the in-and-out contours of a classic baking potato. The hair-do he favoured was a flesh Mohican—hair down either side, a ridge of scalp in the middle. The world he ruled was called NoBell Developments.

"Leslie Queen," said Bell. "Androgynous sort of name, isn't it?"

People who rule worlds often like to waste the time of people who don't, with purposeless, mildly insulting banter. I knew that, so I said nothing.

Or rather, nothing is what I should have said. What I actually said, after enduring twenty minutes of his chitchat, was: "Mr. Bell, I'm seventy-three years old. I wonder which is going to happen first? My funeral, or you getting to the point."

Bell laughed. "That's funny," he said. "I like a guy who speaks his mind." Then he stopped laughing, and his face rearranged itself into a frown. "No, wait a minute, correction— I *don't* like a guy who speaks his mind. I was thinking of my brother. *He's* the one who likes a guy who speaks his mind. I'm the one who demands total subservience at all times. Is that understood, Mr. Queen?"

I didn't desperately need the money. My police pension paid my rent, kept me in whisky and aspirin.

Fact was, I could retire any time I felt like dying.

I didn't need the money, but I needed the work.

"Look, Mr. Bell, you think you have a problem and you think you need a private investigator to solve it for you and you think I'm the one you need. I've no idea about the first two, but you're right about the last one. So tell me what you want me to do, and we can move on to the part where I quote you twice my usual fee, you accept it without demur, and I go away cursing myself for not quoting treble."

He reached into a desk drawer, and brought out a red plastic document folder. "Take that away with you. Read my problem, solve it, and then present me with an invoice for treble your usual fee."

"Treble?"

"Treble."

I picked up the folder, and went away cursing myself for not quoting quadruple.

The folder contained what such folders in such circumstances always contain: a sad story about a spoiled child and a puzzled father.

Castor Bell, nineteen-year-old millionaire's son, worked in a pub in Willesden popularly known as The Morgue. Old-fashioned sort of place, the kind they used to call spit and sawdust. I didn't see any actual sawdust, which was a pity: it could've helped soak up the spit.

I'd never met Castor's mother, but I could see straightaway that he must take after her, in looks at least, because he wasn't ugly. Which, according to my theory, meant he'd never rule the world. But then, if your father's a millionaire, who cares?

I folded myself onto a bar stool, took off my hat, ordered a light and bitter, and lit a cigarette. Castor drew half a pint of flat bitter into a dirty glass and put it on the counter in front of me, next to a warm bottle of light ale.

"You do sandwiches?" I said.

He shook his head. "Sorry."

"Thank God for that." That won me a smile, but not much of one. About as much of a smile as it was worth, I suppose. The beer tasted worse than it looked, and smelt worse than either, so I decided to hell with the subtle approach. I cut to the chaser. "Give me a scotch, will you, Mr. Bell?"

He didn't react to my naming him, didn't react at all, which was how I knew he'd noticed. "Any particular scotch?"

"Whichever one comes in a clean glass."

He gave one of those small, upper class laughs, the sort that sound like a cat starting to cough up a hairball and then losing interest halfway through. "We don't stock that brand," he said, serving me a Bell's from an optic. "But don't worry. Alcohol kills germs."

I said nothing. I was too busy figuring a way of getting the whiskey inside me without my lips touching the glass.

"So. You work for my father."

"Today, I do." I swallowed my disinfectant like a brave boy. "You going to tell your father I've been drinking on his time?"

Castor pushed off from the counter, and went to serve a middle-aged man at the other end of the bar who was drinking draught Guinness and wearing a suit and tie. The suit and tie told me he was the poorest man in the pub: he'd sold or lost all his clothes except those he'd be buried in. From the state of the suit, he'd already been buried in it once or twice.

"I'm not going to tell my father anything," said Castor,

while he waited for the Guinness to settle. "Because I'm not going to speak to him." He used a palette knife to decapitate the pint, topped up the glass, and left it to settle again. That touched me—here was a kid taking the time to do a job properly, even when it was a crap job in a lousy place.

"He just wants to know if you're all right," I lied.

"Yeah! Like giving a shit about me is his specialist subject. Forget it, Mr. . . . ."

"Queen," I said, and showed him one of my business cards. I didn't give him the card, because I hadn't got many left. My printer died last Christmas.

"You really a private investigator?" He studied my grey hair and my cheeks that met in the middle and I knew what was coming next. "No offence, man, but aren't you a little, you know, *elderly,* for that line of work?"

"Would you rather I drove a bus?"

Castor was really staring at me now. "You an ex-cop?"

"Very," I said.

"You believe in justice?"

"I'm in favour of it. I don't know if I believe in it."

He rubbed at his short, streaked hair, with long, soft fingers. "Jesus, what a weird planet. You ever get that feeling?"

"No," I said. "But then, I was born here."

"My shift ends in an hour. Could you wait around? I want to show you something."

It was two things. A building and a beautiful girl. Castor was in love with them both.

"Isn't it stunning?" he said. "Rossland House. Built as a private residence, two hundred years ago. Since then it's been a hospital, a school for paupers, a private house again, and now it's empty. Seriously neglected. But isn't it fantastic, Mr. Queen?"

"It's fine," I said. In a general way, I approve of buildings. They keep the rain out.

The beautiful girl, a tall, poised redhead, had been introduced as Vanessa. No last name was offered, and I didn't ask for one because Vanessa's eyes said she'd prefer it that way. It seemed a small price to pay for having such a creature hold one's gaze.

"Castor's father plans to knock it down," she said. "Can you believe that?"

"Just barely."

"To build a video superstore," said Castor. "Isn't that an incredible waste?"

"I'm with you there, son," I agreed. "Who needs to rent films, when you can see them on TV for free?"

Castor shook his head. "That's not what I meant—"

"Mr. Queen knows that, babe." Vanessa laid a hand on his arm, and just for a moment I hated him. "He's teasing. Aren't you, Mr. Queen?"

"It's not a joke!" said Castor. "And a lot of local people agree with us, they want to turn this into a community centre. Don't you see? We can't just sit back while he reduces a wonderful, rare old building like this to rubble!"

"Well," I said, "rubble is his business. It's how he made his fortune—a fortune that'll be yours one day. He hasn't dispossessed you yet."

The boy turned away, obviously struggling with an impulse to hit me. I didn't wait around to see if he won.

I went home and changed my shirt, then spent the rest of the afternoon running errands for an old person, the old person being me and the errands including a urologist's appointment. It was late evening by the time I again unlocked the door to my two-room flat.

I stood there for a moment, trying to remember whether I'd left the light on when I went out. Maybe I had: my memory isn't what it used to be. Nor are my teeth, though my hat hasn't changed much.

I was still standing there, in doubt, when a man came out of my bedroom, carrying a small, black gun in a large, red hand. He was a big man, but not so big he couldn't get through the door. He was also ugly, but he didn't look like someone who'd ever ruled any world larger than a three-man prison cell.

"You're Queen," he said, covering me with the gun while he locked the front door.

"I already know that," I said. "So if that's all you came to tell me, I'm afraid you had a wasted journey."

He blinked several times, as he tried to work out what I was talking about. It occurred to me that this might take a while, and I wished I'd thought to bring along a puzzle-book.

"I get it," he said at last. "A smart-aleck."

"And for that you're going to kill me?" I said, sounding tougher than I felt. Or feeling tougher than I sounded. One of the two.

"Nobody said I should kill you, granddad, just give you a message."

"I hope you've got it written down, Mastermind. Otherwise, it'd be quicker to kill me. And kinder, too."

He hit me with his empty hand. It hurt, but not like the urologist.

"Forget about the Bell kid," he said. "Drop the case." And then he left, before I could ask him how come his lips moved when he was thinking, but not when he was talking.

It had been a long day. My old CID sergeant used to say, when he was dying of the cancer, "Better another long day than that final long night." He had a point, I suppose, if points are your thing.

I poured a drink, drank it, swilled out the glass, got undressed and got into bed, huddling against the cold of the sheets, ready for another long night. Not *the* long night, just *a* long night, but a long one, nonetheless, in a long, rarely-broken series of long ones.

Either the whisky or my clean conscience did the trick, though, for as soon as my head touched the pillow, a dark, swirling tunnel opened up before me, and I found myself falling, falling, falling into a great void of utter blackness.

I don't know if I snore or not. I didn't used to, but these days, who's to say? I know I don't dream any more, haven't done for years. I think that's because, everything there is to see I've already seen with my eyes open.

The hammering on my door probably hadn't been going on for more than an hour by the time it woke me, and it probably wasn't any louder than a slow avalanche landing on a thin roof.

I managed to get the door open before it fell in, and my dressing gown on before I fell out. Two victories in one morning, and I hadn't even had my first cigarette.

Two police officers fell through the doorway. The one that was plain-clothed, middle-aged, short and female looked at my dressing-gown, spent a few moments disliking it, then looked up at my face and shook her head, sadly.

"You're Queen," she said.

"I already know that—" I began, but she was too busy to catch the rest of my act.

"Detective Inspector Murray." She flashed a card, and signalled to her young PC, who headed for the bedroom to begin silently dismantling the detritus of my life.

"If I ask if you've got a warrant, will you hold it against me?"

No reaction.

"I used to be in the job myself," I said, "if that makes any difference."

She looked at me with slightly more contempt than I deserved. Not a lot more, but enough to hurt. "Makes a difference to your pension," she said. "Makes sod-all difference to me."

"Want to tell me what you're looking for?"

"The blunt instrument," she said her back to me as she searched my bookcase for blunt instruments.

"What blunt instrument?"

"The blunt instrument you used to kill Mr. Wise."

"Who's Mr. Wise?"

"The man you killed."

I'd heard better patter on Talent Nite at the Three Feathers. I put a hand on DI Murray's shoulder, and said, "Look, will you just tell me—*Oof!*"

She swung a sharp elbow into my groin and I suddenly decided to sit down on the floor and wheeze. It's not exactly yoga, but it's good for focusing the mind.

"This Mr. Wise," I said, as soon as I was able. "Where was he found? And if you say 'Where you left him,' I'm going to report you to the Commissioner for wearing red shoes with a blue skirt."

She didn't smile. I don't just mean there and then—my guess is she didn't smile ever. "Back of this building. In amongst the dustbins."

"He still there? May I peek?"

She scratched her ear, thinking about it. "Why not," she said eventually. "With any luck you'll get his blood on your shoes and I can nick you for that."

We left the Boy Scout hunting for porno under my bed, and walked down to the back yard. As advertised, a large corpse lay partially hidden by a wheeled bin. Mr. Wise, *AKA* the thug from last night.

"You know him?" She watched my face for a reaction. Call me conceited, but I like to think she watched in vain. "He's known to us. Desmond Wise. Odd-job yobbo for a gang-connected demolition firm called Coots. Mean anything to you?"

I didn't answer. At that stage I wasn't sure which bits I was going to end up lying about. "He's been cleaned up," I said, pointing to some bloody smears on his bomber jacket.

"The killer took his cash and cards, is what we assume. Then wiped the jacket for prints."

I leant forward and sniffed. Something was prickling my nostrils—something other than blood and garbage, and the everyday stink of the city. Which, come to think of it, *is* blood and garbage.

"What?" said Murray. "You half man, half bloodhound?"

"I smell beer."

"So? He was a man. All men smell of beer."

"Yeah," I said. But he hadn't smelt of beer when he'd left me. Besides, the smell of beer wasn't on him. It was on his jacket. "Tell me, Inspector, now that we've become so close. Why'd you knock on my door this morning? Apart from a kinky thing you have about seeing old men in their pyjamas."

"Anonymous phone call. Gave us the meat." She nodded at the late Mr. Wise. "Gave us you for a garnish."

"But you didn't like the phone call much, which is why you didn't bother with a warrant."

She made no comment to that. I'd have fainted with shock if she had.

"So I'm free to go? Assuming your toy-boy hasn't found

too many gore-encrusted candlesticks in my sock drawer."

She shrugged. I walked. I was almost out of sight before she called after me. "If you're thinking of going abroad, do me a favour."

"Yes?"

"Make it somewhere that has the death penalty."

I found my coat and hat amid the rubble of my rooms, and used the drive to my client's house on Hampstead Heath to sort things out in my aching head.

At the end of my first day on a new case, I get home, not to a roaring fire, but to a dim thug named Wise who warns me off the aforesaid case, acting on behalf of person or persons unknown. He leaves my flat, is somehow persuaded by further person or persons unknown to add a visit to the communal dustbins to his tour itinerary, where he's introduced to a blunt instrument or instruments unknown. Wise cracks, or at least his skull does, and someone (presumably the second person unknown; see above) dials three nines and drops my name in a CID duty officer's ear.

All pretty simple, really, as puzzles go. I'd figured out who by the first traffic lights. Why kept me busy until I reached the clean streets of Hampstead.

Mr. Bell, once I'd been admitted to his presence, spent five minutes telling me how he never saw anyone without an appointment, and then another five, making sure I understood the gist of the first five. When it was my turn to speak, I kept it brief. We both had busy schedules that day.

"I met your son yesterday. I also met his girlfriend. This morning I met a copper called Murray, and last night I met a Coots enforcer named Wise. My hectic social life would be the envy of many a retired person."

I had his attention. "This chap Wise. What did he want?"

"Who cares? He's dead."

"I see." From Bell's face, he clearly thought I'd killed Wise. I let him think it.

"So if you want to know what he was up to, you'll have to ask Mr. Coots himself. You do have his phone number, don't you?"

"Seems I have no secrets left, Mr. Queen. Yes, Coots and I do have an . . . ongoing business relationship."

"The sinful art of merger, right? No, don't bother not answering, I'm really not interested. I'll take my cheque now, and see myself out."

He laughed, as hard as he could manage. Sounded like an asthmatic lizard. "Why would I pay you, Queen? I hired you to stop my son sabotaging my plans for Rossland House. In the event, all you seem to have achieved is a—a—"

I filled in the blank. "A gang war, Mr. Bell? As a result of which, I'd guess, you and Coots won't be developing Rossland House. So your son won't have anything to sabotage. So I've done my job." I stood up. "So I'll take my cheque."

He looked pale and shaken, serving beer at the far end of the bar. She looked pale and composed, sipping gin and tonic at the near end. They both looked young and rich. I looked old and poor, but I am blessed with a ruddy complexion.

"Does Castor know your surname?" I asked, keeping my voice quiet and my face loud.

She didn't hesitate. If she was truly as hard as she thought she was, it was a miracle her arse didn't break the barstool. "Not my real one, no."

Castor had spotted me, and hurried over, his lips trembling, his death-white face sweating.

Vanessa Coots hopped her hips up onto the bar and kissed

him on the nose. "Gotta go, babe. Mr. Q's giving me a lift to the Tube. Phone you, OK."

In the car she asked the final question first, which showed a certain chutzpah, if nothing else. "Are you going to turn us in?"

"No," I said.

She exhaled loudly, like a seal dying of a puncture wound. "Thanks, Mr. Q. You're a sweetie."

"And you're a lying, scheming, ruthless murderer. But you are a quick worker, I'll give you that. How did you find my address?"

"Castor followed you on his bike," she said, neither boasting nor apologising, "while I phoned that sucker Wise, told him I had orders from Dad. Did he remember his message long enough to deliver it? *Durrr, lay off de kid, mister.* Honestly, that man was a joke!"

"Yeah. A regular scream." Rich, beautiful, and cold. What a combination. "So I get the word from Wise, he exits my building, you *'pssst!'* at him from a shady corner, he shambles over, and Castor caves his head in."

"I do my own caving-in, thank you very much. I'm very strong, you know. I work out. I could crush your ribcage with these thighs." She hitched her skirt an inch. It was a long inch, and taking my eyes off it wasn't the easiest thing I ever did.

"I get the blame for putting out Wise's bright lights, the Bells and the Cootses go to war, the merger's off—"

"And Castor's lovely building is saved for the nation." She beamed at me, sitting on her fingers like a clever little girl.

"The building, yeah. That's Castor's motive. As for you— well, the fact that if it all works out you get rid of your father, his top people, and his main rival all at once, that's just coincidence. Pity you had to wipe the blood off that leather jacket with one of Castor's bar towels. Pity my sense of smell isn't as geriatric as my knees."

She giggled. "It was either a smelly old bar towel, or a three-hundred-quid silk scarf. Still, doesn't matter, does it, Mr. Q? Because you look on me as the daughter you never had, so you're going to let me get away with it."

"Believe me, Vanessa, if I could send you down without dropping Castor in it, you'd be wiping fingerprint ink off your fingers right now."

She looked puzzled. "Castor? What's that sorry little boy to you? You're not gay, I can tell you're not."

I didn't bother trying to explain—to her or to myself. "Let's just say there aren't enough barmen left in London who know how to serve a pint of stout."

She shrugged. She couldn't care less. About me, or pints of stout, or sorry little Castor.

"There are three conditions, Vanessa. You get Castor out of the country—today. As soon as he's safe, you tell him who you really are. After that it's up to him."

"Yeah, can do," she said. After a moment she added, "And the third condition?"

Had I said three? I could only think of two. "Right. Third —you pay for transforming Rossland House into a community centre, out of your sweet little allowance. Got it?"

"Deal. You're not making an heroic effort to prevent a gang war, then?"

"The more of your kind that kill each other, the more champagne I'll drink."

I pulled in by the Tube station, kept the engine running. Vanessa ran her tongue lightly across her lips. "Is this the bit where you crush me to your manly chest and kiss me like I've never been kissed before?"

"It might be, but luckily for all concerned I have the wrong teeth in today."

"Your teeth look fine to me. I mean, they look false, sure, but they don't look as if they'd fall out or anything."

I gave her a smile. Nothing special, just an old one I didn't use any more. "If your teeth don't fall out it doesn't count as kissing, Ms. Coots. Not in my book."

She pouted fake disappointment. "Oh I get it. You're one of those tough guy detectives who thinks girls are a nuisance."

"Not to me they're not," I sighed. "Not in years."

I started to lean across her to open the door on her side, the way tough guys do, but then I thought better of that—I don't have such long arms. I let her open the damn door herself.

Then I went home, drank a significant amount of whisky, and failed to sleep; safe in the knowledge that tomorrow would be another long day. Or else it wouldn't.

★ ★ ★ ★ ★

Writing this story was a lot of fun—and that's something you won't often hear me say!

In 1999 I was asked to contribute to a special Raymond Chandler tribute issue of the crime fiction magazine *Shots*. Who could resist? Not me; not someone who has spent most of his life waiting to be told "I don't like your attitude," just so he could reply, "That's all right. It's not for sale."

Obviously, this is an attempt to write a story in a Chandleresque voice, with a couple of twists: the elderly detective (a character who had been in search of a setting for some time), and the fact that we're in London, not California. But I did something else, as well. . . .

I re-read a couple of books of Chandler's short fiction and his famous essay, "The Simple Art of Murder," wrote down as many titles, quotable lines and so on as I could find—and then set about writing a story which could contain them all, whether in their original form or disguised as puns. (For instance, my original title, rejected by the magazine, was "The Smell of Beer.") I can't tell you how many Chandler references are hidden in the text; I suspect there are some that even I've forgotten.

My favourite line in this story, if you're interested, is: "He was a big man, but not so big he couldn't get through the door." That strikes me as gratifyingly close to the real thing. And if you disagree—well, I don't care for your attitude.

DO THE WORLD A FAVOUR

I'd been planning to take my flask of coffee into the station and sit on a bench on the up platform for a while, watching it all go by. I like watching railway stations. I'm not a trainspotter, I just like watching railway stations. The people, the journeys, the swirls of litter and pigeons.

But when a block-shaped, middle-aged woman in a bad hat levered her scowl into the back seat of the mini-cab and shouted *"Driver!"* I took such an instant, deep dislike to her that I thought: well, why not? Could be a nice day for a drive.

"Where to, love?" I said, weaving the taxi out of the car park on to the main road.

"The Pier Hotel. Do you know it?"

"Of course I know it," I lied. "I'm a taxi driver."

She sniffed. "On your break, were you?" she asked.

"No, that's all right. Just stretching my legs."

"It is not all right, thank you very much," she said, turning her face a fraction to the left so that she could look out of the window instead of at the back of my head. "You don't think, perhaps, that this country might be just a little more competitive if people spent less time on breaks, and more time working?"

"Why don't you," I replied, not loudly but clearly, "hurry up and die and do the whole world a favour?"

She was already sitting upright, she obviously wasn't one to slouch, but now she sat even uprighter. "I beg your pardon?" Ridiculous expression: it means *you* must beg *my* pardon.

We were passing along the seafront, going in the wrong direction for the hotels, though she was too paralytic with anger to have noticed yet. I pulled into the kerb, stopped the car and got out.

The old bag banged about the backseat for a bit, before re-establishing her centre of gravity. "What on earth do you think you're doing?"

Two kids—teens, I suppose, early twenties—sat slumped against the beach railings, a plastic co-op bag spread on the ground between them. I looked at them, looked at their bag: at a rough calculation, it contained about fifty pence. I groped a fiver out of my shirt pocket, and stuck it in the girl's hand. The kids looked at me, for the first time.

"Cheers, mate," said the boy, with a shuffling movement of his mouth that might have been a smile when he first got it, several birthdays ago. It made his upper lip split and bleed a little.

The girl was still staring at the money, trying to remember what she was supposed to do with it, and it wasn't until I'd got back into the cab, just before I closed the door, that I heard her say, "Yeah, cheers, mate."

I clunked my seat belt, and looked in the rear-view mirror. "Sorry to keep you, love. Just on my break."

The old bitch selected an unamused smile from her armoury, deployed it, and said, "You won't be expecting a tip, then."

"What, not even so close to Christmas?"

"There would seem little point in my giving you my money only for you to pass it on to beggars."

"True," I said. "I take your point. You could give it to them yourself, couldn't you, and cut out the middleman?"

She redistributed her buttocks, huffily. "I do not give to beggars."

"Never?"

"Not under any circumstances. Begging is not an activity I wish to encourage." I could sense her nodding in the back there, congratulating herself on her good judgment.

"Still," I said—and then paused. Thing is, I'm a quiet chap generally. My ex-wife says I'm the sort who only talks when I haven't got anything to say. But this conversation interested me. "Still, homeless people, eh? I mean, you can't just walk on by, can you? Can't pretend they're not there."

She leant forward. "There didn't used to be any *homeless people* in this town. *Homeless people*—" a phrase she pronounced with a mixture of disdain and disbelief "—used to stay in the cities. I just don't know what went wrong with this country."

I could tell by the tone of her sigh that she really didn't know. Incredible. "Well, I'm only guessing, madam, but could it perhaps have something to do with a complete absence of compassion on the part of the better-off?"

She found another humourless chuckle, this one a sort of swallowed woof. "Compassion!"

"You're familiar with the term."

"I'm familiar with the disease, certainly. But I'm glad to say it is not one from which I have ever suffered. I reward prudence and punish improvidence. I do not waste my energy on compassion. Why don't these people get a cloth and a bucket and knock on a few doors?"

"If they came to your door, unwashed and tatty and clutching a smelly rag and a bucket of dirty water, you'd pay them to clean your windows?"

"Don't be ridiculous! Where are we going?" She was

looking past me, through the windscreen, where town was giving way to country.

"Nowhere you'll enjoy," I replied—and then, quickly, before she could digest my words: "Those kids looked like they should be worrying about puberty, not where their next meal's coming from."

It worked. "I don't appreciate sexual language, thank you," she said, sitting back in the seat.

"You got a husband?"

"Of course."

"Poor bastard."

The old bitch crossed her legs and lounged, almost happily. "So, your compassion extends to my husband? You don't hate him the way you hate me."

Ah, she wasn't stupid, then. Good: the really stupid feel no fear. "Most fascists are women," I explained. "Women of your class never have to earn a living, so they spend their entire lives sitting around polishing their ignorance. At least their husbands see a tiny bit of the world, get their hard edges knocked off a bit."

"That's how you imagine me spending my days—eating caviar and truffles, scolding the maid and reading detective stories? How very old-fashioned!"

"Disillusion me."

"Not that it's any of your business, but as it happens I am a district councillor and a magistrate."

I should have guessed. "Well, well. Prejudice combined with power. You really are the complete item, aren't you?"

She shook herself, sat forward again. "I asked you where we were going."

"And I answered."

"This is not the way to the Pier Hotel. Don't try to cheat me, driver. Better men than you have tried that, and lived to regret it. Now, where do you think you are taking me?"

"I told you, love: you're going somewhere you don't want to go."

"*Where?*"

I adjusted the rear-view mirror. I wanted to be sure she could see my face properly. "Death, death, death," I said, grinning with all my teeth. "Death, death, death. You get it? You're going to die."

She stared for a moment (not in fear yet, more in silent repetition of her family motto: "I just don't know what went wrong with this country"), and then, predictably, began to rattle at the door handles.

"No good," I said. "You can't open them. They can only be opened by the driver, you see, to guard against fare dodgers."

With outrage gouged from her soul, she snarled, "Do I look like a fare dodger?"

I gave her an appraising once-over. "No, to be honest you don't. What you look like, since you're asking, is an evil old bag who deserves to die." And after that she didn't say anything for quite a while. In fact, she went dead quiet; that is, after the screaming.

"Why?"

I let her have a come-on-girl-don't-be-coy look, via the mirror. "Why do you think? I'm a serial killer. I pick up evil old bags in my mini-cab, drive them out to remote spots, and rip 'em. You must have heard, it's been in all the papers."

A little later, she said, "There wasn't anything in my paper."

"*Daily Mail?*" I said. She nodded. "There you are, then. I don't approve of the *Daily Mail*, left them off the press release list."

She started to nod again, then changed her mind and shook her head instead. "You're no serial killer."

"No? What am I, then?"

"You're just an absurd little man who feels sorry for scroungers, and resentful of success. Like all your sort. You are a little man who is about to lose his job."

I took the next corner at a speed that sent all the dash-board clutter into orbit. Crumpled tissues, Fox's Glacier Mints and evil old bitches flew about the taxi's interior like confetti in a crematorium chimney. As she climbed back on to her seat, I turned round in mine and stared at her for three, four, five, carelessly suicidal seconds.

"And you, my lovely, are a fat lady who is about to lose her innards."

You don't have to travel far round here in search of a lay-by or quiet country track, the sort where you can conduct private business uninterrupted and unobserved. Indeed, the one I eventually chose, or happened upon, might have been de-signed specifically for the purpose. I half expected to see one of those signs, you know, like the one that says "P On Verge Only," except this one would have said: "Area Designated for Torturing Fascist Bitches to Death. Please Leave this Facility as You Would Wish to Find It."

I found it by instinct. I used to drive round those roads all the time in the old days, roads that are only between some-where and somewhere else unless you're a vet, or a tenant farmer, or some kind of tradesman.

I saw a turning, confidently swung the cab into it, and within seconds we were hidden from the entire known uni-verse. The tractor tracks beneath us were hard and dry and antique looking. The hedges either side of us almost met at the top.

I was invisible. To everyone except her.

★ ★ ★ ★ ★

"You can keep the hat," I said.

"The hat?" She shivered. "Why the hat?"

"Because you look like shit in it."

At first, when I'd got her out of the car and told her to take all her clothes off—take them off and burn them—she'd still been a magistrate coping calmly with a difficult journey. "And how do you think you are going to persuade me to do that?" she'd asked.

"With this," I said, and smacked the baseball bat down on the car, leaving a dent in the roof.

Her hand went to her mouth, slowly. "My God. You really are a serial killer."

I had to laugh at that. "Christ alive, I was right: you wouldn't know real life if it tore your tits off and fed them to you. Which it's about to do, as it happens." I hefted the bat. "Every taxi driver carries one of these, these days. Even in a content little town like yours."

Now, fifteen minutes further into eternity, she stood there trembling, truly terrified at last, and wearing nothing but her stupid hat.

I left her there for a moment, while I sat in the driver's seat, with the door open, and smoked half a cigarette. I knew she wouldn't try to get away: lady magistrates in seaside towns don't run away from serial killers, dressed only in crappy hats. They just don't.

I crushed the cigarette out against my shoe and flung it into the bushes, walked up to the old bitch and said, "Move."

"What do you mean?"

"You're in the way," I told her. I got back into the car, closed the door, and started the engine. I rolled the window all the way down. "You're in the way, I can't get the car out with you standing there. Move."

She dropped to her knees, holding her wrists together down by her belly button as if they were tied. Which they weren't. She was shaking violently, and crying dryly. "What do you mean?" she said.

"Look, I'm sorry," I said. "I just can't do it. Just haven't got the backbone, I suppose. Must be your lucky day."

"What do you *mean?*" she howled.

I beckoned. "Here—come here. That's right. It's a cold day, but I'm not going to kill you. I *am* a serial killer, you see, but I'm on my break. Here, take this." I still had my flask, untouched, so I poured her cups of coffee, one after the other until the flask was empty, and stood over her while she drank them.

Irrelevant, I suppose, but I couldn't help noticing that she didn't say thank you. That kind has no manners.

It was all lies, of course. All of it, all lies. I'm not a serial killer. Me? You're joking! I don't even use slug pellets. Or *didn't,* when I still had a garden, still had a house of my own. I'm squeamish, that's the truth.

It was all lies about the taxi, too. It was a taxi, yes, but it wasn't my taxi. I'm not a taxi driver; used to be an electrician. Now I'm—well, I'm just me.

As I said, I'd been planning to sit in the station, sip my coffee slowly, but then she slammed into the back seat, shouting *"Driver!"* And I glanced at the open driver's door, saw the keys hanging from the ignition—I'd seen the driver jump out a few seconds earlier, to use the loo, perhaps, or get a sandwich from the kiosk—and I thought, why not?

So, all lies. The taxi, me being a serial killer. It was even a lie when I told her I wasn't going to kill her. I have killed her. I gave her all my coffee.

Well, why not? I still have the flask. I've plenty of pills back at the bedsit, plenty more coffee, I could always make up another batch tomorrow, go back to the station, sit for a while watching the trains and the pigeons and the people rushing around.

I wonder how far she walked before she died?

★ ★ ★ ★ ★

Some people think this story (which first appeared in 1994, in *Crime Yellow*, edited by Maxim Jakubowski) is a rather nasty piece, but to me it's just an old-fashioned story of good triumphing over evil. Depends on your point of view, I suppose.

What really pleases me about it, anyway, is that it has *clues* in it. The plot actually *works*. That's a rare pleasure for me; I am not one of the genre's great plotters. Usually what happens is that I get almost to the end of a story, and suddenly realise that I don't know who was killed, by whom, or why, or how the man with the orange beard and the three-legged dog fits into the thing, if at all. And that's when the sweaty work starts.

That's more or less what happened here—except that when I read the story back I found, to my astonishment, that its conclusion was a genuine twist, decently prefigured by subtle hints. Amazing. Evidently, my subconscious had known what was going on, even while my conscious mind was as clueless as ever. (Just as well *one* of us was paying attention). It made me feel like a proper mystery writer.

That was in 1993. It hasn't happened since.

NOT A MINUTE ON THE DAY

On the ninth day of the general strike, Winston Churchill died of a heart attack, quite without warning. Less than a week later, I found myself just as unexpectedly back in my old job.

Well, almost my old job. In 1919, I had been a bobby—now I took the oath as Detective Inspector Enoch Jones, of Gloucester CID. Advancement is there for the taking in times of great change, of course. Even so, I wonder if my loyalty to the trade union cause would have been so rapidly and extravagantly rewarded had it not been for the violent and potentially embarrassing death of a young undergraduate named Ernest Scott.

Churchill! Will history ever show us a Briton more universally loathed by his countrymen? Hated with a passion by the working people, for the divers cruelties and injustices he inflicted on them over many years, and in which he seemed to take such a wicked delight; and at the same time despised by his own class as an unprincipled and reflexively treacherous career-chaser.

Even so, he shall have his small place in history. With his death the heart went out of the government's fight. It was no secret that Prime Minster Baldwin and his allies in the Cabinet had all along favoured a peaceful settlement to the dispute, and that Churchill had been almost alone in raising the banner of "victory at any cost."

Until his death, the "class war," as the *Daily Mail* called it, had been going badly for the unions. The Trades Union Congress was ill-prepared, ill-led, and divided, and rumours of its imminent surrender circulated freely. But the removal from the scene of Winston, that unyielding militant, coincided with a devastating fire (which may or may not have been started deliberately) at the BBC's Savoy Hill studios. The wireless, which by now reached almost two million listeners, had committed itself enthusiastically to the bosses' cause.

These two events, along with an incident in Hyde Park in which soldiers, apparently fooled by fog into believing that they were under attack by armed Russians, had opened fire on a peaceful crowd of protesters, changed everything.

Baldwin, having lost his voice and his strong right arm, lost his nerve. "The master manipulator," as the miners' leader A. J. Cook put it, "became the missing rudder of a rudderless administration." He sued for peace, but by now it was too late; now it was the strikers who had nothing to gain by compromise. Their leaders knew that by the end of the week they would either rule the country—or be in prison awaiting the rope.

On the eleventh day of the strike, units of soldiers began to defect to what the pro-government press called "the rebels." When Winston's body set sail for burial in his mother's native America, Baldwin & Co. sailed with it. Nothing was said, but it was understood that they would not be coming back.

Councils of the People (the unions were careful to avoid calling them *soviets*, the words of the Bolshevik litany still having power to horrify, since the time of the Zinoviev forgery) were being established throughout the industrialised areas of Britain. In a manner surprisingly straightforward—or should we say predictably British?—these swiftly took over the running of essential services.

At tea-time on the fourteenth day, J. H. Thomas, on behalf of the TUC, informed the nation that the emergency was at an end, ordered all trades unionists to report to their places of work, and announced that a general election would be held as soon as practicable. Meanwhile, delegates from each Council of the People would convene to elect the officers of a Council of Councils which would govern *pro tem* (along with various bishops and suchlike sympathetic respectables), in the name of "New Labour;" a term carefully chosen to distance the new government in the minds of the people from the failures of the *old* Labour gang of 1924.

"A policeman, yes. But are you a proper policeman? Hmm? Or are you a plainclothes Bolshevist?"

"I'm afraid I don't understand the question, Sir Randolph," I lied. I kept my voice soft. A man who has lost his son deserves respectful treatment, whatever his class.

"Don't understand the question? I'm sure!" Randolph Scott stood at one end of the great fireplace in his large, dusty, drab, unmistakably wealthy drawing room (Reception room? Parlour? Not "front room," I imagine). I stood at the other, hat in hands. He was a tall, thin, clean-shaven widower in his mid-fifties, with a full head of white hair. I was a tall, thin, clean-shaven bachelor in my mid-thirties, with a full head of dark hair. We made a fine pair of bookends, or fire-dogs.

Scott ruined the symmetry by walking up to me and staring right into my eyes. "How long have you been in the police force?" he demanded.

"I joined before the war, sir," I replied. It wasn't quite the whole truth. I had joined the Metropolitan Police in 1913, but I had been expelled from it in 1919, following the second of that year's two police strikes. I had been a die-hard union man, one of thousands "cleansed" from the force when the government made it illegal for police officers to be members of independent trades unions. Those who stayed, who agreed to renounce their industrial freedom, had been rewarded with generous pay rises and a ten pound bonus. Such a huge lump sum had proved an irresistible temptation to most. Since then, I'd been unemployed, save for occasional casual work running errands for the railway unions.

My economical reply seemed to satisfy Randolph Scott (I was damned if I would refer to him as *Sir* Randolph in the privacy of my own thoughts).

"Very well," he said, inviting me to sit at last. "No offence, Jones, I hope. But in these terrible days one doesn't quite know that anyone is who he appears to be. Days when a *collier* gives orders to a king . . ."

"Quite, sir," I replied, neutrally. "May I offer you my condolences on the tragic loss of your—"

"Yes, yes," he said, waving my words away with a busy hand.

"I believe your late son, Ernest, was a student?"

"He was up at Oxford, yes," Scott corrected me. "Final year."

"And what did he study there, sir?"

Scott gave me a look of scorn. Clearly, my question had been a *faux pas* in some way that I could not fathom. "You're not a university man yourself, Inspector." This was not a question; though I had lived all over England since my schooldays, my country accent still told him all he needed to know about my upbringing. "You'll not find the answer to Ernest's death in Oxford, man!"

"No, sir?"

"No sir! Look to the Bolshevists, look to the rebels, look to the strikers!"

I wondered if Scott was one of those rich men who believed that the new government of workers was a temporary aberration, sent by God to test the faith of decent Englishmen for a few weeks or months before the natural order of things inevitably reasserted itself. From our brief acquaintance I thought it likely; more likely than that he was of the other type, those who were already adapting, learning to live with the changed circumstances, holding on to as much as they could, whilst quietly awaiting the next spin of the wheel of fortune.

"I understand, sir, that Ernest took an active part in the recent events?"

"He did his duty, Inspector, as Scotts have done for centuries. Sadly there are others of whom the same cannot be said, but Ernest did his best to defend his king and country against atheists and traitors."

"And what form did this duty take, specifically?"

"My son drove an omnibus in London, under the auspices of the Organisation for the Maintenance of Supplies. He did, Inspector, what any decent young man would do—he answered his country's call, and it cost him his life."

In the course of the great strike, there were very few instances of real violence committed by the men against their opponents—to the disappointment, one must imagine, of some factions on either side.

I did hear of one disgraceful attack by shoeless malcontents upon the dignity of the state, though to describe it as violence would probably be to exaggerate it. A mounted troop of Special Constables—made up of young financiers and retired military fox-hunting gents, sworn in for the duration of the emergency and armed with sawn-off polo sticks—was tricked into entering a narrow and stinking back alley in

Whitechapel, where the contents of several dozen chamber pots were emptied over their heads from the windows above.

It is said that one young wag, his steel helmet dripping with all manner of filth, which had been especially reserved for the purpose, turned to his companion and remarked: "The socialists are right, damn it: these people *should* have indoor plumbing!"

But murder, as an act of political revenge? No, I could not believe that.

For the most part, the strikers did not particularly resent the blackleg role played in the strike by their "betters." Rather, they took it as natural that the class which had most to lose from democracy and equality should do everything in its power to prevent the rise of organised labour. Besides which, even from the perspective of a hungry picket, there was something just a little enjoyable about watching one of one's betters struggling to control a bus or mail van, his (or indeed, her) face running with the sweat of unaccustomed work.

Nonetheless, someone had killed the Oxford undergraduate, Ernest Scott. If not an angry member of the lower orders, then who?

I travelled up to London in most pleasant fashion, in a First Class railway carriage, which was empty of First Class people. Or indeed, of any others: old habits die hard, and the guard, to my amused surprise, questioned my right to place my plainly proletarian bum upon such plushness, until I scared him off with my papers of identification.

The Civil Service had destroyed thousands of documents relating to the strike once it had become clear that their old masters were on the losing side. All was not lost, however, as good luck and a lot of polite questioning led me along a trail of Old Etonians and Oxford graduates (there had been no purge of the Civil Service; this *is* Britain, don'cha know!), stretching from the Organisation for the Maintenance of Supplies (where hung a pencilled sign: "Under New Management."), via the Foreign Office, to the Ministry of War. There I met a short, plain, young woman, whose name I heard as Anna Hyphen-Hyphen, and whose brother's flatmate's cousin had been a hunting associate of the late Ernest Scott. A small world, these people had lived in.

Miss Hyphen-Hyphen furnished me with an introduction to the hunting associate himself, a red-haired young layabout named Piers. From his animated manner, I deduced that he was fonder of cocaine than was likely to be good for him. Not that it was any of my business.

"Ernie did the driving," Piers explained, as we sat in his Chelsea flat. The place was evidently too small to house a manservant, so the cup of tea I had hoped for did not materialise, and I had to make do with gin, served with Indian tonic water. I found it rather medicinal. An acquired taste, no doubt.

"And you were the conductor?"

"That's it, spot on. Piers the Clippie—that's me. Tremendous fun, best laugh we'd had in ages! They should throw one of these general strike thingies every year, if you ask me. Makes a change from slaving away in my old feller's place."

"Your old feller . . . ?"

"Stockbroker, you know. Dullest business on God's earth." A stray thought blundered, almost visibly, into the young man's impressively empty head. "I say, don't get me wrong, the old feller's awfully good at it. Everyone says so. I can give you his card, if you like—he says there's never been a better time to invest. As soon as this lot's sorted out, prices are going to go through the roof."

I smiled. "I fear my salary doesn't run to much in the way of stocks and shares. The odd horse now and then, that's about my limit."

"Oh really? Right you are." He grinned vacantly, rubbed his nose on his sleeve, and gulped down about four inches of his cocktail.

"The bus you were assigned to—it ran from Hampstead to the West End, is that right?"

"Oh, absolutely. All the way. Broom-broom-broom. Splendid fun! I begged old Ernie to let me have a go behind the wheel, but you see, the thing is, I can't actually drive. So that was that. Not that I minded, as it turned out. Poor old driver misses out on all the pretty girls, you see!"

"Ernie was a good driver, was he?" According to some reports, more buses were put off the road by incompetent volunteer driving than by mass picketing.

"Rather, I should say." The ginger hair, thinning already, flapped as Piers nodded his bulb-shaped head. "At least, we didn't have any accidents. Didn't squash any pedestrians, you know."

"You were on this bus from Day Two through to Day Seven of the strike, is that right?"

"If you say so," said Piers. "I'm hopeless with details, but that sounds about right."

"And during that time did you meet with any trouble?"

"Trouble?" said Piers.

"I mean, did you run into much opposition? From the striking transport workers, or their supporters."

"Oh, right, see what you mean. Well yes, actually, we did. The last trip we took, we were just coming up to Cambridge Circus, and suddenly we were surrounded by—God, I don't know—*hundreds* of working chaps. You know, all shouting and pushing up against the bus."

"The enemy within," I muttered, remembering a phrase of Churchill's from his propaganda rag, *The British Gazette.*

"Well absolutely," said Piers, refilling his glass and emptying it again, virtually in the same movement. "I don't mind telling you it all looked a bit hairy for a mo. I mean to say, there were a lot of these chaps, and they were jolly determined. Still, fair's fair, they were perfectly decent about it as it turned out. One of them climbed up into the bus and told us, quite politely, that he'd really rather we didn't go any further. Well, of course, the way they had that old girl hemmed in, we couldn't have moved if we'd wanted to. I mean!"

"So what did you do?"

"Well, *moi,* I was all for abandoning ship. I mean, fun's fun, but no sense banging your head against a brick wall, is there? In any case, it was getting on for lunchtime, so I went up front to old Ernie and I said, 'Come on old thing, let's see if the club's open'."

"The club?"

"Oh, the Tiger Club. It's a sort of, you know, club thing. You probably wouldn't know it," he added unnecessarily, "it's more for the younger set, if you see what I mean."

"And was Ernest ready for lunch, too?"

Piers sniffed vigorously, hoping, I suppose, to inhale a few specks of powder left over from his last indulgence. "Well, no, not entirely. He took the whole thing rather seriously, you know, this bus-driving lark. He seemed quite put out at the way we'd been brought to a halt. Said something about not being dictated to by a mob of stinking scarecrows. Well, as I say, *I* was most impressed by their good manners. Sort of chaps you'd be glad to have beating for you, if you see what I mean. But Ernie—well, he was a sound fellow, but he was rather the type who let people rub him up the wrong way."

"Was there a confrontation?"

"Wouldn't call it that, exactly. But old Ernie did get down from his cab. Wanted to speak to the chaps, I suppose."

"And did he? Speak to the chaps?"

"Dunno, really. He sort of disappeared from view, do you see? Into the crowd."

"Was there violence? Were blows exchanged?"

"No, good heavens, no. The chaps were rather taken by surprise, I think. They let him through. I saw Ernie put out a hand, to tap this one chap on the shoulder, sort of get his attention, but the fellow turned away, wouldn't speak to Ernie. And then I lost sight of him. Well, I wasn't going to sit around doing nothing for the rest of my life, so off I went to lunch. The old club was open for business as usual, which was nice."

"And did Ernest turn up for your next driving shift?"

"No, afraid not. Never saw him again," said Piers. "Probably went on strike, what?"

"The man that Ernest wanted to talk to," I asked, "was this one of the ringleaders?"

Piers shrugged. "Didn't seem to be. I didn't get a proper look at him, but I mean to say—ringleaders would be at the front of the crowd, wouldn't they? Bound to be, sort of thing."

As I took my leave of Piers, he belatedly asked: "I say, do you happen to know? How did Ernie die?"

"Strangled. His body was found in a ditch not far from his family home."

"Oh I say! Poor old Ernie. Strangled—not much fun, what?"

"No," I agreed. "Not much."

I had one more call to make in London, at Scotland Yard. George Lake had been my sergeant when I'd been in the force before, in Islington. Never a union man, I wasn't surprised to discover that he'd been transferred to the secretive, nameless unit of the Metropolitan Police which dealt with monitoring and undermining "subversives" —the name people like him give to those who would rather fight than starve.

We had been on different sides in 1919, and we were on different sides now. The difference being that now I was a detective inspector, and a man in tune with his times. And poor old George was still a sergeant.

"Good to see you again, George," I said, as we shook hands in his tiny office.

"Likewise, Enoch," he replied, just as insincerely. I'd get no "Sir" from him—men like George Lake wouldn't accept defeat even if you hanged them. In a way I admired him for that; better a principled enemy than a fair-weather friend.

"So," I said, looking around the broom cupboard. "What have they got you doing these days?" I am not a cruel man, but I couldn't resist asking that question.

"Administration," he said, his tone daring me to make something of it.

I took the dare. "Ah," I said. "The fast track to promotion, eh?"

My banter found no echo. "What do you want from me, Enoch?"

"I'm investigating a murder," I explained. "And I have reason to believe that one of the people involved might be known to you." I was guessing, more or less, but I wasn't going to say so to Sergeant Lake.

"Known to me? In administration?"

"Known to you," I said, "previously."

I gave him a name, and George smiled for the first time. Smiled the way a wolf might smile, to greet the scent of injured prey. "You want to watch it, Enoch. Take care. It's not friends in high places who count in the long run, you know—it's *enemies* in high places."

He told me what I needed to know, however.

The road from Gloucester city to Randolph Scott's stately pile passes through several small villages and hamlets known to me from my youth. They haven't changed much in three decades. Few of their inhabitants enjoy the benefits of mains—electricity, gas, or even water. When they fall ill, they are more likely to see a priest than a doctor, since the clergy charge less. The success or failure of what New Labour calls "This great project" will be judged by many of us according to how much transformation we see in places like this, amongst people like these.

"I need to speak to your son, Sir Randolph. Your *other* son." I was aware of how absurd that clarification sounded, but also aware that many of the rich were quite obsessed with spiritualism, and this was no time for misunderstandings.

"My—my other son?" Scott didn't sit, though his legs begged him to. "I have no other son."

"And yet you *had* another son, Sir Randolph. Didn't you? Harold. He'd be a few years older than Ernest. I remember his name appeared frequently in the local paper at one time—giving out Sunday school prizes, and so on. Don't hear much about him now, though. Why is that?"

"I tell you again," said Scott, rousing his blood for one last burst of *ancien regime* defiance. "I have no sons, sir! One is dead, and the other ought to be."

"Nevertheless, Sir Randolph. If you would be kind enough to fetch Harold—unless you'd rather I did?" I really didn't know whether or not the boy was at home, but hoped that my threat of tramping my working class boots around the

House of Scott would bring a truthful reply, either way.

In the event it did better than that. Just as Randolph started to say, "Harold is in Europe," another voice joined us.

"If you truly wish me dead, Father," said Harold, stepping elegantly through one of the several doorways which led off from the Scott's front room, "then all you need do is wait, I'm sure, and let justice take its course." Tall, thin, he was a younger image of his father, as I could plainly see despite the bruises and healing scars which covered his face.

"Justice?" Randolph snarled. "They'll not hang one of their own!"

"As a matter of fact, Sir Randolph," I offered, "I have heard that the government plans to abolish capital punishment."

"Then they are fools as well as devils," he said, and turned his back on us.

I placed my hand on Harold's shoulder and said: "Harold Scott, I am arresting you in connection with the death of your brother, Ernest."

"*In connection?*" sneered Harold. "Inspector, I killed him."

One thing I'll say for the upper crust—they confess in style. "Because he saw you in the rebel crowd that stopped his bus, yes?" I'd assumed that Ernest had leapt from his driving seat to confront someone he recognized; if he'd merely wanted to remonstrate with an anonymous revolutionary, he wouldn't have needed to wade into the crowd. And when I'd asked Sergeant George Lake whether any of Ernest Scott's known associates had been suspected subversives, the name Scott itself had immediately rung a bell in George's memory.

"I wasn't happy to be spotted, I admit," said Harold. "But it needn't have been the end of the world. At least, as far as I was concerned. Sadly, Ernest never did have much of a sense of proportion. When I came down here to visit dear old Pater—to tap him for some funds, if you must know—Ernest insisted we go for a walk, to talk things over. The conversation was not to his liking, I fear, for he attacked me, as you can see from my face, and in the ensuing struggle . . . well, he died, and I didn't. Self-defence, you see."

"That'll be for the court to decide," I said. There was still one thing I wished to get clear—as a trade unionist more than as a policeman. "Did the TUC know that Soviet agitators like you were—"

"Soviet?" Harold laughed, an affected, effete laugh. "My *dear* Inspector! Bolshevism is dying even as we speak, a Jew-raddled old whore. My allegiance is not to Moscow, but to Rome."

For a moment I wondered what the Catholics had to do with anything, and then I understood. "Mussolini?"

"You've heard the name, at least. Jolly well done, Inspector. And you shall hear it again. The Reds won't hold power for long—they lack the guts, you see, the guts and the breeding. While the old ruling elite is too decadent to reclaim its throne." He smiled, like a young man who knows everything and hears nothing. "Which only leaves us, d'you see? From chaos comes order. The future, Inspector, is Fascist."

As I settled Harold Scott into the back of my official car, his father tapped me on the shoulder. He looked pathetic, as a man well might who has lost both sons in one moment.

"They're all Bolshevists," said Randolph Scott, "whatever they call themselves. But Ernest—Ernest was a good boy, a fine man. You'll see, Inspector, they'll build statues to that boy one day. He'll be remembered as a hero one day, you see if I'm not right."

That seemed unlikely to me, but it would have been cruel

to say so. *Let the dinosaurs die in peace,* I thought, as I drove my prisoner through the English countryside in spring. *Let them die in peace, in a world they didn't make and cannot comprehend.*

★ ★ ★ ★ ★

This was my first attempt at a historical story, and my first alternative history story. Putting those two together with a murder mystery seemed like an interesting idea, when I was trying to come up with a contribution to one of Martin Edwards's CWA annuals (*Past Crimes,* 1998), which that year had a history-mystery theme. The great advantage of alternative history, of course, is that no one can tell you you've got the details wrong.

I've long enjoyed reading about the 1926 strike, and hearing anecdotes about it from family elders, and I enjoyed writing about it. I'd like to return to Enoch's universe some time—though I'm not sure how big a market there is, globally speaking, for alternative history-mysteries concerning the British labour movement in the early years of the 20th century.

FAMOUS FOR ONE THING

Very late one night in August 1976 I was mugged, at Temple Meads railway station in Bristol.

I say mugged—"beaten up" would probably be more accurate. I had a Wimpy burger and a bag of chips in my hands, and they took those; and I was wearing a Somerset cricket hat, and they took that. But they didn't take my wallet—I didn't *have* a wallet, but even so they didn't take it, if you see what I mean. I did have a wristwatch, and I probably had two or three pounds in my pocket, and they left me those, too, so you couldn't really call it a robbery.

There were four of them, three boys and a girl. Teenagers, same as me. White, same as me. Been drinking, same as me.

When they'd finished—I suppose the whole thing took about three or four minutes, perhaps less—I sat on the ground for a while, feeling dizzy, sick, lonely, all that sort of thing. Generally sorry for myself.

And then my train came in, and I got on it. It was the last train of the night, you see, so I got on it and went home.

At that time I was living in a youth hostel. I didn't have a roommate; paid the extra two pounds a week for a "single," liked my privacy even then, in those gregarious years. I was certainly glad of it that night, as I sat on my bed, looking at my wounds in the shaving mirror. They were singularly unheroic wounds. Cut lips, swollen eye. Nose bleeding, but not broken. Teeth were intact, although they ached like hell.

I've often tried, but have never been able to remember exactly what it was I was doing that night, before going to the station to catch the last train. Or who I was doing it with. I've simply forgotten: didn't get a knock on the head or anything like that, no selective amnesia; I just forgot. Doesn't matter, of course, couldn't be less important—it's just annoying, has annoyed me all these years.

So sometimes, when I can't sleep, I like to recreate that evening in my mind—as it might have been, as I hope it was. Nothing fancy. Nothing ambitious. Just—a crowd of lads and lasses, some in pairs, some in the process of pairing up. Meeting in a cafe, on to the pictures perhaps, or a bowling alley if we had the money, or more likely just a mooch round a couple of record shops. Then the pub, naturally, and ending up with a bag of chips, or—did we have kebabs in those days? I forget.

These days, I don't get out much, don't see many people, except professionally. I find my own company dull enough, don't require the tedium of others. But twenty years ago I had a pretty lively time, I think. I *think*. As far as I remember.

I remember the station, though. Remember waiting there. For some reasonless reason, every detail of that bleak scene is still almost tangibly clear in my mind. The coin-in-the-slot chocolate dispenser that didn't work—they never did in those days, I wonder if they've changed? The bags of cold chips lying around the platform, their innards hanging out—abandoned half-eaten as their owners' trains arrived. I remember the platform's sole occupant, other than me; an old woman with four suitcases and a walking stick.

I remember the smells, and the noises, and, of course, I remember the sound and the sight of the gang as it approached.

I remember that as if . . . not as if it were yesterday. As if it were now.

I didn't go to the police that night to report the mugging, or to anyone else. I can't say exactly why not, all these years later, except that—well, that's not what seventeen-year-old boys do.

So what did I do, instead of filling in forms at the local nick? I did what you might expect a mildly pretentious, moderately sensitive, halfway educated seventeen-year-old to do.

I wrote a poem.

I called it "Mugged." Just a working title at first, but in the end I found—as is so often the way with working titles—that I couldn't really improve on its plain, descriptive brevity.

I suppose I had an idea—or more likely, an instinct—that writing about what had happened to me would be therapeutic. Would help me to move on from an unpleasant—but after all, not terribly significant—experience.

And it might have worked. If it hadn't been for that bloody competition.

I was never much good at school. I don't simply mean not much good at lessons, or not much good at games. I mean that the whole occupation of "schoolboy" was one for which I was hopelessly ill suited. If I'd been born an adult, I'd have got on much better.

The one thing I could do was write poems. Don't know where this ability came from. Nobody else in my family has ever written more than a postcard home from Ibiza. But this . . . knack, I think you'd call it, did go some way to making up for all the other things I couldn't do. Kept the teachers off my back, to some extent.

Because poetry is one of those odd activities for which it is possible to win praise at school, even though it is never likely to be of any use to you in the grown-up world. Bit like throwing the cricket ball on Sports Day, or being Joseph in the nativity play.

So poetry became a habit with me. And as luck would have it—good or bad, you decide—there was a notice on the board at the hostel the day after I'd been beaten up, advertising a national youth poetry competition. First prize one hundred pounds.

I sent off "Mugged," forgot about it, my cuts healed, and two months later I got a letter saying I'd won first prize, and inviting me to attend a prize-giving reception, in the presence of various poetic dignitaries, at some gentlemen's club in the West End of London.

And the rest . . . is the rest.

The club, a grey, labyrinthine building somewhere off Whitehall, was quite impressive, but rather shabby. The poetic dignitaries were rather shabby, but not at all impressive.

I'd never heard of any of them. I didn't follow poetry, you see. It wasn't a hobby of mine, or an interest, or a passion. It was just something I could do. I was there strictly for the white wine and canapés—well, you'll eat anything at that age, won't you, provided it's free—and, of course, for the hundred pounds.

I read "Mugged" to the assembled old folks, pocketed the check—easily the biggest I'd ever seen—and I was just getting ready to leave, filling my pockets with food, and wondering if it would be possible to slip a bottle of wine up my sleeve without anyone noticing (and whether it would *matter* if anyone noticed in any case, because wasn't that how poets were supposed to behave?), when an elegant woman of about thirty-five took hold of my elbow and said

"I'd like to talk to you, Peter."

She was quite attractive, in a cynical sort of way—and I suppose, with hindsight, that I must have been quite attractive, too. Well, I was seventeen, wasn't I? How much more attractive than that does anyone need to be? To anyone who is no longer seventeen themselves, I mean.

Kate was a feature writer, for one of the Sunday broadsheets. The short version of what happened next is that she drove me back to her flat in Kentish Town, where we drank the two bottles of wine she'd helped me pinch from the poets, and where she interviewed me about my poem. In that order.

I never saw Kate again—I suppose there's no shortage of seventeen-year-old virgins in London at any given time—but she did write a nice piece about me. I sent copies back home and to friends far and near, and had almost forgotten about it when I received a letter, forwarded on from Kate's office, from the artistic director of something called the Non-Theatre in Soho. He was looking for plays by young writers, he'd read about me in the paper, and would I like to meet up some evening?

Well, I thought: why not? You spend a lot of time at that age thinking *Why not?*, don't you?

And that's how the play came about—as easily, as innocently, as that. In the late seventies, you may remember, angry youth was still quite "in;" provided it was being angry in the theatre, that is, and not on the streets of dimly-lit housing estates. And if angry was what they wanted, well I could be as angry as the next youth, given sufficient incentive.

The chief incentive in this case was a three-month writer's contract which, considering my modest lifestyle and even more modest expectations, prompted me to pack in my office job.

Yes, I had a job; they weren't quite as rare in those days as

91

they became later. It was a *job,* note, not a career. In fact, it was so boring that I exaggerate only slightly when I say that I can no longer remember what it was.

I rented a bedsit in Bristol's student-land—well, you can't expect award-winning writers to live in youth hostels, can you?—and wrote the one-act play in one week flat. And that was with spending every lunch time and evening in the pub. Piece of cake, writing plays: almost as easy as writing poems; just involves a bit more typing, that's all.

I called it . . . "Mugged." Why change a winning formula?

It was, by the standards of the Non-Theatre, a smash hit. Not only did people come to see it—the theatre had a maximum audience capacity of forty-two, or fifty-seven, if you didn't worry too much about the fire regulations—but, more importantly, it got reviewed. By Kate—who was very kind—and even by several people I'd never slept with.

The theatre's artistic director got a better job with another company—one with a salary which more closely matched his pretensions—and I got interviewed three times on the radio and twice on the telly.

I was almost famous. One of the interviewers asked me if, considering the way things had turned out, I wouldn't rather like to find the thugs who'd beaten me and shake them all by the hand.

I didn't answer that.

The book came next.

It's still in print, if you're interested. A classic of its kind, according to the arbiters of such things. It was called, once again, "Mugged," and it consisted of my poem, and the script of my play, photographically interpreted by a number of brilliant, cutting-edge, challenging, angry, young, art school poseurs. It was a Significant Statement on Urban Violence and

Disaffected Youth. Or something. Got reviewed absolutely everywhere.

Best thing about it was that, since I'd already written the play and the poem, I didn't have to contribute any labour towards this project other than a spot of proofreading.

Got a lot more than one hundred pounds for that job, I can tell you. *Lot* more. Moved out of the rented bedsit, bought myself a studio flat. In Clifton, actually. Very nice.

This is going to sound like boasting, but I swear it's true: I actually cannot recall which came next—the BBC2 *Play For Today* version of *Mugged*, or the off-Broadway production of *Mugged*. Or was it the graphic novel? Either way, *Omnibus* did me in about 1992, and the Channel 4 feature film is due for theatrical release sometime next year.

And then, just this morning, I had the most extraordinary phone call. From the girl. The girl who had been in the gang who beat me up at Temple Meads railway station in August 1976.

Could have been a con, of course, don't think I didn't think of that. But—well, all I can say is, she convinced me. Something about her voice, what she said, the way she said it. And she knew some details of the incident which I've never used, anywhere. She knew, for instance, that I had burst into tears and begged for mercy.

What did she want? What she wanted, basically, was a piece of the action. She was very sorry about what had happened, naturally, very ashamed, but—well, you do things when you're young, don't you? Daft things. Bad things. And, hey: I hadn't done too badly out of it all, had I?

I couldn't argue with that. I still have the flat in Clifton, and another in West London, handy for the TV studios, but I spend more time in my cottage near Gloucester. I live very comfortably; I am a well-known and even respected writer. I haven't done badly.

Whereas she—Janice—has a handicapped child, no job, no money, no husband. And she was just thinking: hey, if I, Peter, were to acknowledge her—anoint her, publicly, as one of the protagonists in that seminal literary event, that defining moment at Temple Meads—she might be able to make enough out of her notoriety to get some special help for her child. Could we meet up? To discuss all this, and so that she could look me in the eye and say sorry, so that we could let bygones be bygones.

What could I say?

A lot, actually. I could have said: Yes, you've got your problems, but I've got mine. It's twenty years since I last travelled on a train. For twenty years, I have slept with the light on. And in twenty years, when I have slept I have only ever dreamed one dream: of waiting for a last train that never comes.

I haven't done badly. I have money and fame and leisure and security. And if I could change one moment of my life, it would be that moment, Janice—the moment of our one and only meeting.

I was never an ambitious boy, but I think—if I had ever thought about it at all—I would have wanted more from life than this. Would have wanted to put more *into* life. I've never grown up, Janice—I've just got older.

I told her, "No, sorry, no chance of getting together. Far too busy, working on lots of new projects, you know."

A lie, of course. I have no other projects. I only have, have only ever had, "Mugged." That one, brief, nasty episode is, in a very real sense, the beginning, the end and the middle of my entire existence.

No: the true reason that I won't, can't, daren't meet Janice is a much more basic one. It is this: I know without doubt that if I ever did meet her, I would try to kill her.

★ ★ ★ ★ ★

I was a punk rocker in 1978, so I didn't take much notice of Paul Weller's band The Jam, beyond despising it for its unpunkness. A decade or so later, I bought a compilation tape which, despite advertising itself as "the best of punk," included a number of what were, in my stern opinion, non-canonical items—such as The Jam's "Down in the Tube Station at Midnight." The more I listened to this song, the more I admired it. It's a dark little story, told with wit and rhythm, in which the narrator gets beaten up on the Underground.

Wouldn't it be strange, I thought, if you wrote an autobiographical story like that when you were not much more than a kid . . . and it turned out to be the one thing you were known for, throughout the rest of your life? Just then the phone rang; Hilary Field at the BBC in Bristol had a spare slot for a short story, and that fine actor Chris Harris was standing by. Did I have anything suitable? "I've got just the thing," I said. "Give me a day or two to type it up."

It was first broadcast in July 1996, and has never been in print before now.

NOWHERE TO BE FOUND

The last word he said to me was "topography."

When the phone rings late at night I always look at the clock first and *then* answer the phone. A sign of chronic pessimism, according to my last girlfriend—always anticipating bad news. Well, there's an obvious retort to that.

"Jerry? You've got to come and get me. How soon can you get here?"

Seven minutes past two in the morning. It was November, and big winds were herding hailstones against my bedroom window. "Alan? What do you mean, come and get you? Where are you?"

"I'm at home, of course. Wake *up*, Jerry. I really need your help here, man. I'm leaving Jackie, right now, and I . . . are you *awake*, Jerry?"

"I'm awake, calm down. You and Jackie are splitting up? What's happened?"

"I'm leaving her, you've got to come and get me. You should be here in under two hours if you put your foot down. OK?"

He rang off. I sat there thinking for a while, feeling slightly sick from a combination of the sudden awakening and the beer I'd drunk the night before. Then I had a shower, got dressed, and set off for Wiltshire.

The drive down from London took me just over three

hours door to door, in terrible weather and over unfamiliar terrain. Alan was hopping by the time I arrived.

"Where have you *been*, Jerry? I've been leaving messages on your bloody machine for the last hour and a half." He didn't shake hands, or smile, or even say hello. He'd been waiting for me outside the cottage, at the far end of what was little more than a mud lane. I was impressed with myself for having found the place; I'd only been there once before, when I'd helped Alan and Jackie move in.

"Got here as quick as I could, mate," I said, opening the car door but not getting out—I wasn't sure if I was *supposed* to get out or not. "So, what's the plan? Got any luggage?"

"Yeah. Wait here." He turned and walked back up the path towards the cottage. His back was as soaked through as his front. He looked freezing cold, but he also looked as if he was unaware that he was freezing cold.

Just as he reached the cottage door, I called after him. "Alan?"

He paused without turning, his irritation visible even through that weather. "Yeah?"

"Good to see you, mate."

"Just wait there, OK?"

I waited there, the car radio playing, the motor thrumming, for five minutes before I eventually thought, *Sod it, the least I'm due is a slash and a cigarette.* I got out of the car, walked up the path and knocked on the door. *Cup of tea and a piece of toast wouldn't hurt, either.*

Jackie opened the door. She yanked it towards her as if it was sticking from flood damage, then let her hand slide off the doorknob as she turned and walked away. She didn't look at me.

I followed her into the kitchen, at the back of the house. She was wearing a dressing gown over a pink nylon nightie.

Blue nylon slippers. The general air of someone who has realised that giving up smoking all those years earlier did not, after all, placate the gods sufficiently that they would evermore keep sadness from her hearth. Her face was grey, except where it was red. If a half-decent paramedic had turned up at that moment, he'd have prescribed a dozen full strength fags and a pint of vodka. *Then* breakfast.

"Sorry to intrude, Jackie," I said, from the kitchen doorway. She sat at the table, her back to me. "I just wanted to . . . obviously, I don't know what's going on here, that's your business. I just wanted to use the loo, if that's all right?"

She didn't answer, but then it was a pretty daft question. No matter how much someone's life is falling apart, they're hardly likely to respond to such a request with: "No, you bastard! Go and do it on the compost heap!"

I had a pee, a bit of a wash and brush up, drank some cold water from the tap in cupped hands; I didn't reckon a pot of tea and a plate of scones were going to be appearing in that kitchen any time in the near future.

I could hear Alan still moving about upstairs, so I sat down at the kitchen table. Eventually Jackie did look at me, but she needn't have bothered: there was nothing in the look that said anything.

"Well," I said. "This is a bad day."

She began crying, silently, her eyes fixed on mine. Now that she'd started looking at me, it seemed, she couldn't stop.

"Do you know where I'm taking him to, at all?" I asked. "Because I don't."

She shook her head, very short, surprisingly careful shakes, and wrinkled up her face and cried some more. I'd thought she *wouldn't* speak, but I realised now that she couldn't speak. Another gulping of sobs caught her by surprise, like sudden vomit. She clamped two fingers over her lips, as if fearful that if she allowed her mouth to fall open even a crack, all her vitals would slip-slide out and pool around her feet.

I reached over and patted her arm, which didn't seem to help enormously. I didn't know what else to do—I hardly knew the girl, for God's sake, I'd only met her once before. Twice, maybe.

Footsteps clattered on the carpetless stairs, and Alan appeared. He was carrying nothing but a duffel bag. "What are you doing here? I said wait in the car."

"I needed to use the loo," I said, and immediately wished I hadn't offered him an explanation at all. The rude, ungrateful bastard! It wasn't even as if we were close friends. We were *old* friends, certainly, known each other forever, and I loved him like a brother. But your brother isn't usually your closest friend, is he?

We went out and got into the car. Neither of us said goodbye to Jackie, and she didn't speak to, or look at, either of us. It was still raining. People often say, "I must be mad to do this," but at that moment I really did wonder if I was actually mad. Or if one of us was, anyway.

"Is that all you've got? One duffel bag?"

Alan looked down at the duffel bag between his knees. "That's it," he said. He didn't seem inclined to say more, so after a brief pause to search for loose cigarettes in the glove compartment (there weren't any), I fired up the motor and headed off in what I hoped was the direction of the motorway.

"You got any smokes, Alan? I ran out on the way down."

He shook his head. "I packed it in."

"All right," I said. "I'll stop somewhere. Anyway, be breakfast time soon, right?"

He wasn't talkative—he wasn't in fact saying anything,

which is untalkative by anybody's standards—but that didn't surprise me. He'd been with Jackie a good few years, on and off, and any break-up that occurs in the early hours of the morning is, by definition, a sudden break-up.

I couldn't keep silent, though. Not on a journey of that length. Not with no sleep, no breakfast and no cigarettes. Time dragged. So did distance—I didn't know my way around there, the weather was no better, I was driving slowly.

Every minute or so I'd say something like "Well, this is a bad night," or "Maybe things'll look better in a day or two." But I had to be careful what I said, careful not to sound too disapproving. Because the truth was, I *did* disapprove. I didn't know the ins and outs of this particular situation, obviously, but I couldn't help feeling that a man like Alan, who'd had three wives before he was thirty, was more often than not likely to be the author of his own misfortunes.

And he knew I disapproved. Which is why I tried to keep things light.

"So where is it I'm taking you?" I said, after a few more silent miles, and with the bloody motorway still playing hide and seek in the country darkness. "Back to my place, is it? Because that's fine if it is, goes without saying, my floor is your floor. Might even find you a spare pillow if you're good."

"Stop here," said Alan, and I was so shocked that I obeyed him immediately. He started struggling with the seat belt. Its release catch had always been dodgy.

"What's the matter? You feel sick?"

"You can drop me here," he said.

I peered out of the windscreen. I couldn't see much because of the weather, but I got the impression that there wouldn't be much to see even on a clear day. Just hedges and fields. No houses for miles around. "Alan, we're in the middle of nowhere. We're on a road with no pavements, for

God's sake. We're on a road with no pavements, it's raining and we're Londoners."

He freed himself from the death-trap seat belt, and started struggling with the door handle. A deeply non-mechanical man, Alan; never learned how to ride a bike, let alone drive a car.

"Look, Alan, I don't feel happy about leaving you here. I mean, at this time of night, in this weather—what are you going to do, hitchhike? I can take you where you want to go."

He got out of the car, slung his duffel bag over his shoulder, and ducked his head down to speak to me. He started with a half-smile, the nearest thing to a friendly face I'd seen all night. "No, don't worry, Jerry, I'm not hitching. I've got a friend lives just near, I'll crash there for a day or two while I sort myself out."

I'd never seen anyone lie so obviously in all my life, but what could I do? "What's this place called, then?" I asked, trying for a tone somewhere between skeptical and joking.

Alan shook his head. "I don't know it by name, exactly, I just recognize the topography." He began walking in the opposite direction to the one in which the car was pointing. Within a very short time he was invisible.

I called after him, "I can drive you to your friend's house, that's no problem," but I don't know if he heard me.

What could I do? You can't force a grown man to stay in a car, no matter how hard it's raining. As I leant over to close the door that he'd left ajar, I spotted a cigarette, bent but unbroken, under the passenger seat. So I sat and smoked that, and after a while the sky became lighter and I was able to find my way back to the motorway and home.

It wasn't until three years later that I went looking for Alan. Perhaps I should explain that.

Alan never became a Missing Person, except in the crudely literal sense that he was a person, who was missing. No official body ever listed him as missing, because nobody ever reported him gone. He hadn't had a regular job in years. He had no mortgage, no driving licence, no credit cards, no bank account. Alan Hallsworth was one of those people whose only proof of existence is their heartbeat, who never trouble the computers of the world, either with their presence or their absence.

His parents had divorced when he was twenty, long after he'd left home, and Alan had achieved the impressive feat of becoming permanently estranged from both of them. I remember him boasting to me about that, one sober night. "I have literally," he told me, "*literally* got an address book with no addresses in it." Another night, equilibrium restored by Guinness, he'd changed his mind about that. "I didn't mean that I'd *literally* got an empty address book," he explained. "I just meant that I don't know where my parents live, either of them, and don't wish to know. I haven't actually got a *literal* address book, empty or otherwise. Don't need one—don't know anyone."

His wife, of course, might have reported him missing, but when I once suggested it to Jackie, on the phone, she sounded puzzled. "But I kicked him out, Jerry. I mean, you know, him not being here sort of goes without saying, doesn't it?"

Missing Person, of course, is a definition rather than an occupation, and it's one that not every person fits, even when they do happen to be missing.

And me? I never reported Alan missing because I never believed for a moment that he was a missing *person*. Almost from the start, I thought of him as a missing *corpse*.

Two weeks after my pointless journey to and from

Wiltshire, I still hadn't heard from Alan and I was beginning to get worried. He didn't know many people, and I'd been certain that he and his duffel bag would end up on my sofa before long. After all, where else do you go when you're running away from home but to London? No offence to Wiltshire, but it's definitely a *from* place, not a *to* place.

That was when I phoned Jackie. She was no longer unable to speak without crying, and made it unambiguously clear to me that her marriage, her husband, her husband's duffel bag, and her husband's friends were all part of her past, not her present. Goodbye.

So, I thought: *he must be dead.* If he was alive and well, he'd have been in touch with me. If he was alive and in trouble, the authorities would have been in touch with his wife. Therefore, he must be dead—and undiscovered. A missing ex-person.

As weeks and months passed Alan's supposed death and disappearance faded from the forefront of my mind, the way even the biggest things in life will under the daily onslaught of little matters. I thought of him most at Christmastimes, when he didn't send me a card. He never *had* sent me a card, you see, not once in all his life, and I'd always sent him one, and it had always rankled. But now, I couldn't really blame him for not sending me a card, because there wasn't really much he could do about it.

And then, as the fourth Christmas approached, I suddenly thought: *I've got to know.* Just like that, really: I've got to know. After all, it was my car he got out of.

The drive down still took me three hours. The weather was OK this time, but I still didn't know the way.

The cottage in which Alan and Jackie had served the greater part of their marital sentence was uninhabited now, empty and boarded up. I sat outside it for a while, smoking, listening to the shipping forecast, wondering where to start.

Three years earlier, I'd asked Jackie on the phone "Was there another woman?"

"*A* 'nother' woman?" she'd replied. "There were *several* 'nother' women. But not one that would have taken him in."

If Alan was alive he'd have been in touch. I'd known him since we were both kids, and I don't think there'd ever been a period of three consecutive months during which we didn't speak to each other at least once.

He had been killed deliberately, because if it had been an accident his body would have been found, and word would have trickled through to me eventually, through one twisting conduit or another.

I finished my cigarette, turned the car in the craterous road, and set off slowly to try and retrace the route we'd driven on the night he left. After about an hour of dawdling, reversing, peering and swearing, I gave up. One bit of rural road looks much like another, unless it's where you live.

Once winter's early darkness had turned my mission from futile to farcical, I stopped at the next pub, which happened to be one I'd seen a few hours before, on my drive down. I reckoned it was about ten minutes walk from Alan and Jackie's old place. Their local, by any chance?

I needed a drink. Until that day, I hadn't said the word "murder" to myself—not out loud, so to speak. The logic was solid enough, and had been there all along, but I suppose acknowledging it was just one of those jobs I'd preferred to put off indefinitely, like fixing a leaky tap.

Murder, I thought, as I sipped a pint slowly. In which case, given the truncated nature of Alan's social circle, there could only be two categories of suspect: his wife, or one of his girlfriends. (Not a wronged husband? No—Alan put it about a bit, before, during and after his various marriages, but he never to my knowledge slept with anyone else's wife. "I have my standards," he used to say. "They're twisted ones, I know, but they're the only ones I've got, so I keep 'em.")

In my mind, as I drank, I auditioned Jackie for the part of vengeful assassin. Supposing, when Alan got out of my car, he had walked or hitched back to the cottage. He'd changed his mind; he wasn't leaving home after all. It had just been one of those rows that ignite in marriages, and then burn themselves out. Now I thought about it, his lack of luggage perhaps suggested a certain lack of resolution. You don't walk out of a marriage with just a duffel bag, do you?

All right, I thought, towards the bottom of the beer. He arrives back on his own doorstep, tells his briefly abandoned wife the good news: "I've decided to give you another chance, you lucky cow." So why does she kill him?

Well, for all I knew he performed the same show once a month. Leaving, coming back, expecting (demanding?) gratitude. And this time was once too often. Being left by your husband would be bad enough, I imagined, but being left on a regular basis would be even more humiliating. Worse—it'd be *irritating*.

So much for the wife. What about the mistress?

When he insisted on getting out of my car, Alan had claimed that he was going to seek shelter with a friend. At the time, I hadn't believed him. It had crossed my mind then that perhaps he was going home, and was embarrassed to have me drive him there, but now it struck me that there really could have been a friend. She'd have had long, dark hair and big buttocks, no doubt, as did Jackie, and Susan before Jackie, and the Spanish one, whose name I could never recall, before Susan.

But then, what was the story there? Alan gets out of the

car, walks to his girlfriend's house, says "I've finally left my wife, let me in, it's raining"—and she kills him? No, that doesn't work. All she'd have to say, if she wasn't keen on the idea, was "Grow up, Alan. Go home and sleep it off, kiddo."

By the time my pint was dead beyond doubt, I'd talked myself out of the murdering mistress scenario. Which, unavoidably, meant that I'd talked myself into the murdering missus . . .

I needed another drink, and maybe a sandwich to soak it up. While I was waiting for the sole barmaid to serve a man at the other end of the counter with a bag of peanuts (a transaction which seemed to involve a longer conversation than most people have with their mothers on Christmas Day), I eavesdropped a large, red-faced man with a local accent giving directions to an elderly couple who had wandered into the pub holding a road map upside down.

"Excuse me," I said, when the old folk had departed smiling, with their map the right way up. "You seem to know your way around these parts."

"I should do, yeah. Been running deliveries round here for years. Plus I live just up the road. Why—you lost?"

"Well, not exactly. Look, could I buy you a drink, if you've got a moment? I'd really like to pick your brains a bit."

He shrugged. "I wouldn't say no to a lager top."

We took our drinks over to a table, and I pondered my approach. *I need some village gossip* probably wasn't tactful. I decided to rely on ritual and feel my way.

"Cheers."

"Cheers."

"Jerry, by the way." I stuck out my hand.

"Oh, right. Norman. Cheers."

"Cheers." We drank, smacked our respective lips, put down our respective glasses. I leant my elbows on the table.

"Look, Norman, hope you don't mind me waylaying you like this. Thing is, I've driven all the way down here from London to look up some old friends."

"Round here?"

"Right, yep, just up the road here. Haven't seen them for ages, and obviously I should have phoned first, because when I got to their cottage I found it was abandoned. I mean, you know, actually boarded up!"

Norman shook his head sadly. "Lot of that round this way. No jobs, see?"

"Ah? Right, right. Terrible, really, what's happening to the countryside. But the thing was, I was wondering if you might have known them—might know what happened to them. Alan and Jackie Hallsworth."

He looked at me suspiciously, then, I thought, and I wondered if I'd underdone the subtlety, or whether I was merely receiving the standard amount of suspicion awarded by a villager to an outsider who asks questions. I couldn't tell, having never lived in a village.

Norman took his time swallowing a few mouthfuls of beer before he replied. "Well . . . Alan and Jackie. Yes, I did know them. Not to talk to, like, but to nod to. They used to come in here now and then, weekends and that."

"How long have they been gone?"

"You're an old friend, you say?"

"Yeah, you know, we sort of lost touch. The way you do, you know."

He drank some more, and watched me over the rim of his glass as he did so. "Well," he said eventually. "If you've not been in touch for some while, then you probably won't know. They split up."

"Alan and Jackie?"

"Yeah. Afraid so. Few years ago now, must be."

"Oh God, that's awful! What happened, do you know?"

Norman shook his head. "Didn't know them that well. From what I heard at the time, Alan just walked out one night, and a month or so later Jackie was gone, too. Back to her mother's, apparently. She waited around for a while, I daresay, just to see if he was coming back."

"Which he never did?" I asked.

Norman studied me again, but this time without using the beer as camouflage. His suspicion now was overt, though not, I thought, hostile. "Never saw him again. Took off with one of his women, I suppose. No offence, what with you being a mate of his, but—well, he was a bit of a lad, if you know what I mean."

I couldn't believe my luck. This was exactly the conversation I wanted: a discussion of Alan's infidelities, preferably with names and places. But as I started to assure Norman that I knew exactly what he meant about my old friend's ways, he abruptly stood up.

"Got to be going now. She'll be expecting me back soon." He stuck out his hand. "Nice to meet you. My advice, look for Jackie at her mum's. Cardiff, somewhere, I seem to recall. Can't help beyond that, I'm afraid."

Damn, I thought. I must have asked one question too many. Enough to turn a natural gossip into a loyal neighbour. Even so, I felt that what Norman had said—and what he had presumably left the pub in order to avoid saying—told me quite a lot. Alan was a known philanderer, active locally. He had disappeared, and shortly afterwards, so had his wife.

I left my second pint half-finished on the table, and walked out to my car. I couldn't put this off any longer: it was time to visit the scene of the crime.

Whoever had boarded up Jackie and Alan's cottage—the

landlord, presumably—had done a thorough job. I quickly saw that I wouldn't be able to get into the house without some difficulty, not to mention some tools. For now, I'd have to make do with a quick look round the garden. The body was more likely to be in the garden than the house, anyway, I figured. I couldn't really imagine Jackie burying her husband beneath the floorboards.

There was a fair bit of garden, very overgrown now. Most of the land was at the side of the house, with only a small stretch at the front. The back yard was mainly laid to patio—and that, I remembered, had already been there when Alan and Jackie moved in.

I kept a torch in the car, but not a spade, so a proper search was out of the immediate question. As I prodded around more or less aimlessly amid the brambles and frost-blackened weeds, I felt fear, as well as frustration—fear that I wouldn't have the guts or the constancy to come back again, better prepared. And fear that I would.

To do either would be to confront a question about myself that I would sooner have left unanswered: was I a man who believed that one is obliged to make sense of death? I'd never made, or especially tried to make, any sense out of life. But death, especially someone else's death, was somehow a different kettle of ball games.

"I've got a spade here."

The words, quietly spoken somewhere behind my left shoulder, made me leap, gasp and drop the torch, which landed a few yards away in a patch of mud. Norman picked it up and shone it in my face.

"I saw you here earlier today, sitting outside in your car. I come by once or twice a week, to check everything's still as it was. I followed you around the lanes, and into the pub. I'd have spoken to you if you hadn't spoken to me. And now here you are, back again. Didn't need to follow you this time. Guessed where you were headed."

I cleared my voice before speaking, but still it croaked. "From what I said in the pub?"

Norman dropped the torch's beam from my face, to the ground between us. "Didn't know how much you knew. Still don't know how you found out. But you know something, that's clear." He passed me a heavy, agricultural spade, blade end first, and said: "Over here."

The spot he led me to was deep in a small thicket of horticultural neglect, hidden from any view, not too near the house or the road. I could see his logic. As I took a moment to gather my thoughts before beginning the sweaty task of digging my own grave, I went through the motions of considering my options. What it came down to was this: Norman was a big bloke, a physical-looking man, and I wasn't. I hoped he had a gun, or a blunt object, or at worst a knife. He hadn't struck me as the naturally violent type. If I did what he wanted me to do, I hoped he'd end it quickly. End *me* quickly. If I tried to escape, he'd catch me, and probably finish me with the spade.

That was what it came down to, my last attempt to make sense of death: that I'd rather die by a gun than by a spade.

"It was your wife, then, was it? Alan was seeing your wife?" I was playing for time, of course, but only for more time to rest before beginning the digging. I was too far gone in fear and listless despair to try for a higher prize.

"My wife?" said Norman. "I'm not married. I can't be, see, I have to look after my mum, she's been poorly."

As I turned the first sod, I was thinking: "I don't know that many more people than Alan did. How long will it take them to realise I'm dead?" And I was thinking, if this bloke's a psycho killer, he's a bloody bone idle one. Two victims in three years? You wouldn't think they'd allow it in these de-regulated days. You'd think they'd have got some guy in Korea to do it for half the wages, twice the productivity.

But then I realised that I was making too many assumptions. Norman had only two victims that I knew of—he could have had four hundred that I didn't know of. I might be doing him an injustice; he might be the archetypal New Model Worker. I was pleased to think that. There's comfort in numbers, even when there isn't safety. Stupid, but true. Stupid, but human.

Anyway, I dug down a few more feet, and after a while I unearthed Alan.

"I'm to be sharing then, am I?" I said, putting down my spade. I was quite pleased with that. It showed a certain character, I thought, to go out with a quip on your lips.

Norman reached into his coat pocket. *Gun or knife,* I wondered. Gun, I hoped. Blades are too personal.

It was a mobile phone.

"You call them," said Norman, handing me the phone. "I'm no good at all that."

"Call them . . . ?" My croak became a whisper.

"The police," said Norman. "Would you mind? I get all, you know, tongue-tied. With officials."

I looked at the phone. I didn't know what it meant. I looked at Norman. I didn't know what he meant, either. "You *didn't* kill Alan?"

"I didn't mean to!" he said, his face flushing in the torch-light as if I'd offended or embarrassed him. "You know what these roads are like, round here, in winter. I never even saw him. First I saw of him, was when I stopped and went back to see what the noise was." He choked, snorted his nose clear. "I thought it was a badger."

"When was this?" I said. To my relief, I found that my

hands had stopped shaking sufficiently for me to light a cigarette. I drew the smoke in deep, and felt it save my life. I offered the packet to Norman.

"Ta. I'm supposed to have given up last Christmas, but you know . . . When was it? Three years ago. Found out later Jackie'd kicked him out that same night. He must have been hitching, I suppose, though he was going in the wrong direction, silly bugger. Probably pissed or stoned, he usually was."

He took the cigarette down like an outfielder gulping water. I lit him another. "Ta, you sure you got enough? Ta, then."

"Why didn't you call the police? After the accident, I mean."

Norman shook his head, as if to dislodge the shame from his face. "I'd been made redundant three times in five years. Company I was with then, they've got this policy—you have an accident and you're out. Doesn't matter if it's your fault or not. I couldn't allow it, do you see that?" He nodded towards the open grave. "If I'd lost that job just then, the debt would have buried us. I'm not kidding, me and my mother, we'd have been buried alive." He laughed. "Got the push a year later, anyway. Rationalisation. It's just me and my old van now."

"So you put him here."

"Not straight off. I kept him in my shed for a while, but then when Jackie handed in the keys to this place—well, it belongs to my mum, you see. And I knew we'd not be able to let it again in a hurry, not with the way things are."

I was still holding the phone, and I still couldn't make sense of it. "I thought you were going to kill me, Norman. I thought that was what the spade was all about."

"Jesus!" Norman threw his cigarette away. "Bloody hell, man, where could you get an idea like that? I'm not a nutter!"

"Of course not," I said, quickly. "It's only that—"

"It was you asking questions, see? I mean this—" again he nodded towards the grave—"this was never intended to be permanent. Just until, you know . . . my mum. But then you came down, looking for Alan."

"I don't get it." What I meant was: I don't get why you're not going to kill me. Always assuming you're not.

"I knew Alan and Jackie a bit. More than what I said earlier in the pub. We weren't real mates or anything, but when I came round to get the rent sometimes we used to have a drink, like, bit of a smoke, bit of a chat. So I knew Jackie wouldn't miss him, see what I mean? Even if she hadn't kicked him out, she'd just have thought he'd walked out. He would have sooner or later, too."

True, I thought. Alan wasn't one for sticking at things.

"And I knew there was no-one else gave a shit about him, dead or alive. No family, nothing like that. So I thought— well, bit hard on him, bit hard on me, but no point in making matters worse. It wasn't as if I was causing anyone else pain, do you see? By keeping quiet."

"But then I showed up."

Norman nodded, and tears appeared on his cheeks. "At first I thought maybe you were a debt collector. Child Support, whatever. But debt collectors don't go looking for bodies in gardens. See, if he had someone who cared about him enough to come looking . . . well, that changes everything, doesn't it?" He gave a huge, rasping sigh, and sat down on the wet earth. "You call the police, then, will you?"

The mobile phone still didn't make sense. It did to Norman, perhaps, but not to me. I gave it back to him. I gave him the spade, too.

"You can fill in," I said. "I've done enough digging for one lifetime."

★ ★ ★ ★ ★

When I got home, there was a Christmas card waiting for me. Just one. It had a return name and address on the back: Jackie Peters Hallsworth, Cardiff. I read it without taking my coat off.

"Sorry not to have been in touch for so long," she wrote, "but it's taken me a while to sort myself out. Hope you're still at the same address! I hope also that things are OK with you, and that you might drop me a line some time." Then she came to the point. "Are you in touch with Alan at all? I don't have an address for him. If you hear from him, could you give him my address? Tell him not to panic, nothing heavy, it's just that I feel we have some unfinished business."

I got myself a drink, opened a new packet of cigarettes. Finally I took my coat off, and switched the central heating on.

It had occurred to me during the drive home that the only reason Alan got out of my car on the night he died was that he was being driven mad by my silent nagging. So he'd got out, walked along a country road in the dark, and got himself killed.

"Dear Jackie," I wrote. "It's good to hear from you. I have often wondered what became of you. I'm afraid I can't help you regarding Alan. I haven't spoken to him since the night you and he parted. I have come to believe, Jackie, that it's not always possible to make sense of death—"

I swore, screwed up the letter, and started again.

". . . not always possible to make sense of loss, and that sometimes it's best not to try. It sounds like you've got yourself a life there in Wales, and I truly believe that you should concentrate on the present, not the past. I hope you don't find my advice impertinent. And I do hope you'll keep in touch. There's not many of the old crowd left, we should stick together! With love from Jerry."

I hadn't bought any Christmas cards, so I put the letter in an ordinary envelope, addressed it and stamped it and went out to post it before I had a chance to do a lot of useless thinking.

★ ★ ★ ★ ★

I'm very keen on happy endings. I find that the obligatory tragic endings of what is called "noir" fiction reek of infantile cynicism. In my mind, that's the difference between noir and genuine hardboiled fiction—noir is merely a nihilistic pose, designed to make soft kids feel tough; hardboiled is a way of looking at the world that is wry, weary and without illusions, but which acknowledges that the only rational response to hopelessness is suicide. If you're still here, it means you're still hoping—so stop pretending otherwise, and get on with your work.

The trouble is, a *fake* happy ending is worse than useless; it'll stink the whole place out, like a kipper up a chimney. The correct model, I think, is the mood you'll find in many old blues songs: I'm down, but I'm not dead yet. Since I am rather more fluent on the word processor than I am on the harmonica, the above story is probably the nearest I'll ever get to singing, "I woke up this morning. . . ."

BREATHE IN

I don't think I am a paradox at all, but I am aware that many people would think that, if they knew what I do for a living and if they knew what an ordinary fellow I am in the rest of my life.

Today, for instance, I'm up early because I have an early appointment. But first, I have to call in on Mrs. Winters, the widow who lives in the flat below mine. It's Tuesday, and on Tuesdays she likes me to change her library books. Mrs. Winters reads romance, and is a fussy reader. I have never read a romance, so choosing the right books for her is never easy. The librarian is very helpful, though.

On the way back from the library I pick up some special cakes she's asked me to get from an old-fashioned baker's shop. I don't pry, but I guess that the cakes must mean she's expecting company. That's good: she doesn't see many people apart from me, and we don't get much chance to chat—I'm either shopping for her, or cooking, or putting a new fuse in her hairdryer.

I deliver the books and cakes, and then I really have to motor. The man I have an appointment with is a man of habit. He will be leaving his house, on foot, about . . . *now*.

And sure enough, there he is. I park up ahead of him in this quiet street, and hit him with the car door as he walks past, his nose buried in a newspaper. He's still holding his shin and groaning when I put the chloroform pad over his nose and say, "Breathe in, Mr. Turton."

Then it's into the car, and round to the debriefing centre I've already prepared about a block away.

I work in the information retrieval profession. I earn my fees by scientifically applying pain to certain individuals in order to obtain specific results for my clients, who are mostly semiautonomous government agencies and businessmen. Legitimate businessmen, let me stress; I do not work for gangsters.

The man tied to the chair here today is Mr. Lawrence Turton, a union representative at one of the smaller water companies. Not content with negotiating above-inflation pay deals, Mr. Turton also fancies himself as a whistleblower, and is preparing to talk to journalists about alleged impurities in his company's product—thus, incidentally, putting about two hundred jobs at risk, which tells you how much these union people give a shit about their workmates, for all their big talk.

My clients, in pursuit of their legitimate corporate interests, clearly need to know the nature, scope, and sources of Mr. Turton's dossier. They soon will.

I wait until the subject regains consciousness before unpacking my equipment in front of him. It is important that he witnesses the unpacking—an important part of the process. These are all scientific instruments, specially designed and customised. You can't just walk into a shop and buy these things.

He sees me take out the weighted glove. He sees me take out the precision drill, and the rounded length of wood with the vulcanized grip. When he sees what he probably mistakes for a common car battery, he vomits and I have to remove his gag to prevent him from choking to death.

When we've finished our work, I give him more chloroform ("Breathe in," I say, and he gladly does), and make a quick call on my mobile. Someone else will dispose of Mr. Turton. My business with him is concluded. I am no murderer; I do not kill people. Not even when they ask me to.

Back home, I decide to pop in on Mrs. Winters before I settle down for the evening. You can't be too careful with old people, and I will sleep better knowing that everything's as it should be downstairs.

At first she won't open the door to my knock. Can't blame her for that—I'm always telling her, don't open up until you know who it is—but tonight, even after she does know who it is, she still won't open up.

I have to knock a lot louder than I usually do, and for a lot longer, before finally, grudgingly, she opens the door a crack. She still has the chain on, though.

"Are you all right, Mrs. Winters?" I ask her. It's dark in her flat, I don't think she has a single light on. "Not another power cut, is it? I can take a look if you like."

"No, no," she says. "Everything's fine, thank you. I just have a headache, I'm going to go to bed early—nothing for you to worry about. Goodnight now," and she closes the door. I hear the bolts going back.

I'm up all night. I can't sleep. I am very worried about the poor old lady downstairs, because dark though it was I was still able to see that one side of her face was swollen and one of her eyes was closed.

Someone has hit her. And she didn't want to tell me about it. Which, when you're dealing with a proud, private person like Mrs. Winters, can only mean one thing: family.

The only family Mrs. Winters has is a fat, lazy daughter and a thin, lazy son-in-law. Although Terry and Michelle only live ten minutes drive from here, they never do a thing for the old girl. They don't even visit her, except on every fourth Sunday when they come round for the whole day, and let this sweet, penniless widow wait on them hand and foot and spend an entire week's pension feeding them.

Other than that, the only time she sees them is when they need money.

So here's my educated guess about where Mrs. Winters got her black eye. Terry, or Michelle, or perhaps both of them together, visited her, demanded money, and when she was unable (more likely than unwilling, I fear) to comply, one of them hit her.

That's my guess. But if I'm to do anything about it, I need to know for sure. I am no murderer, but for Terry and Michelle I might make an exception.

At six in the morning, I phone Mrs. Winters. I know she is always up and about by five-thirty at the latest, but the phone rings for a long time before she answers it.

When she does, I speak immediately and firmly. "Mrs. Winters, I know someone hit you yesterday. I know that it was either your daughter or your son-in-law, or maybe both. I'm going to come downstairs now to collect your shopping list, and when I do I want you to tell me exactly what happened."

No coherent reply. Just sobs.

"Mrs. Winters, we can't let this go on. You have to tell me what happened."

"No," she gasps. "I had an accident, that's all, I had a fall. I don't need any shopping today, thank you." She hangs up.

When I knock on the door, she doesn't answer. I thought maybe she wouldn't. She is a very proud old lady; she doesn't like to wash her dirty linen in public. But someone's got to look after her, and that's what neighbours are for.

119

Mrs. Winters has a very good lock on her door—I fitted it for her; there have been a lot of break-ins in this area—but of course I have a spare key, for emergencies.

She's sitting in an armchair, still crying. I don't think she's been to bed; she's still wearing the same clothes from yesterday, and the curtains are closed.

I stand behind her chair, and put a hand on her shoulder. "Mrs. Winters, you have to tell me what happened. You have to let me help."

She doesn't look round. She shakes her head. "I don't want to see anyone today," she says. "Please go."

How can I leave her like this? She needs help, and she hasn't got anyone else.

I move my hand from her shoulder to gently cup the back of her head, as my other hand brings the chloroform pad up to her face. "Breathe in, Mrs. Winters," I tell her.

By the time she comes round she's securely tied to a chair in her bathroom, and there is plastic sheeting covering the floor. She's going to tell me. She *is* going to tell me. And then I'll sort things out and she won't have to be afraid any more.

★ ★ ★ ★ ★

Well, yes, that is a nasty little story, devoid of anything remotely approaching a happy ending, and I have nothing to say in my defence—except that when something works, it works. I don't have any statistics to back this up, but I suspect that very short stories tend to be more unremittingly harsh than longer pieces, since their brevity means that the punch line is disproportionately important. Here, however (in a story specially written for *Hardboiled* magazine), what I was most interested in was the central character: a man who is determined to do someone a good turn, but who is incapable of understanding that human relationships have to operate on a basis of mutuality.

BUT POOR MEN PAY FOR ALL

"A matter for the sheriff, surely?"

"Dead," said Hopton.

"Dead?" said Woodward.

Hopton nodded. "Resulting from the late public differences."

"I see," said Woodward. He and Hopton had been on different sides, at least nominally, of the war between Parliament and the King. Both had survived; both hoped to prosper, now that peace and normality seemed to be returning to the realm. "The sheriff was too old to take the field, surely?"

"Died in the Castle."

"Ah," said Woodward. So the sheriff had been a King's man, killed during the Roundheads' siege, and subsequent ruination, of that local landmark. It was so hard to keep track; the market town in which lawyer Woodward and publican Hopton did their business, had, like so many in the West Country, changed hands often during the past five years. So too, in many cases, had the loyalties of the local merchants and professional men. "The constable, then."

"Dead," said Hopton.

"Oh really, Hopton—is *everyone* in this town dead, except we two?" As soon as he'd said it, Woodward regretted it. In 1642, Hopton had three sons; today he had none. "Forgive me, my friend, I forgot myself. It's just that, well, what with the . . ."

"Late public differences."

". . . late public differences, quite so, and the famine *arising* from the late public differences—it is hard to see how a town built on trade might ever recover." He put a hand up to stroke his beard and then remembered he was shaven. "Was the constable in the castle, too?"

Hopton shook his head. "He died of an appointment."

"An appointment?"

Hopton nodded. "With a rope."

"Ah." That placed the constable's affiliations, then. The only hangings in this town had been carried out by Royalists. "What of the squire? I don't believe *he's* dead. Unless of surfeit; not of rope, musket or famine, for sure."

"He's alive," Hopton allowed.

"Then perhaps—"

"Hasn't set foot outside his library since Naseby. Says if he does, cloth workers will use his books to wipe their arses on."

"Why on earth should he believe that?" No, that was a silly question. People would believe anything these days. Woodward sighed. "I begin to suspect, sir, that if I were to list every man of rank within a day's ride, you would declare each of them in turn to be dead. Is that not so?"

"Dead or fled," Hopton agreed. "Meanwhile, a corpse still lies upon the floor of my inn."

Woodward sighed again. "I suppose you'd better show me," he said.

The Angel had been a traveller's inn for hundreds of years, and was renowned for the strength of its dark, sweet beer. Lately, it had been used as quarters by Parliamentary forces, and then by King's men, and then by Parliament again. For now, with the talk all of settlement and compromise, the Angel was back to being merely a pub.

"Did they give you much trouble, the soldiers?" Woodward asked, as he and Hopton walked over the bridge in the crisp winter sun. He had spent most of the troubled years in quieter parts; explaining, since his recent return, that *"My occasions did not allow me to be much here."*

"The hairy ones, a bit. Not the Puritans."

Woodward nodded. This seemed to be the story almost everywhere. The Saints of the New Model Army—General Cromwell's fearsome military machine—were not, as their forefathers had so often been, pressed unwilling into the service of a great lord. Rather, they were serious of purpose and enthusiastic in manner, since they believed themselves to be doing God's work—fighting for nothing less than the salvation of England. More importantly, in Woodward's view, they were fighting not for a master, but for themselves. Thus, in battle and away from it, they behaved with a degree of unity and discipline unprecedented in English experience.

"That's him," Hopton said, rather unnecessarily, pointing at the corpse on the floor of his back-most room.

Woodward, careful not to drag his clothing in the pool of congealed blood that surrounded the dead man, squatted and observed. A knife protruded from the corpse's belly. "Quite a young fellow. Twenty-five or so, I'd say. Somewhere, a mother is weeping." He straightened up, his knees cracking loudly as he did so. He was not shaped for crouching, but for lawyering. "The first thing is to discover the poor boy's name."

"He is Adam Pretty. I am his younger brother, Edward Pretty."

Woodward looked at the newcomer's long nose, deep-set eyes, and down-turned mouth; and from them, to the corpse. Yes, there was a resemblance. So, too, in the thin, light hair, which on both brothers was rudely chopped in the Puritan style. "I am sorry for your sadness," he said, and after holding his gaze a moment, almost in challenge, Pretty nodded, once. "I am Benjamin Woodward, a lawyer of this town, and I suppose you have met Mr. Hopton, landlord of the Angel. I do not think I know you, sir; you are not from here?"

"From Bath. We were returning home, and broke our journey here last night."

"Returning from where, sir, if I might ask?"

This time, there was no mistaking the challenge in the young man's eyes. "From Putney, Lawyer Woodward."

"I see," said Woodward. He had hoped that this bloody matter would prove to be a simple case of cuckoldry revenged, or of resentment unleashed by ale. Perhaps it still would . . . but all the same. *Putney.*

"You were there for the debates?" said Hopton.

"We were, Landlord."

"Ah," said Woodward. This was looking worse every moment. "You attended the debates in, might I ask, what particular capacity?"

At this, Pretty laughed for a moment; and then, finding himself laughing, wept for a moment more.

Benjamin Woodward had never lost a loved one—nor ever owned one to lose—but he had seen grief before, and was not a cold man. "Forgive me, Mr. Pretty, these questions can wait. Mr. Hopton—might we not move to your private rooms?"

"We might."

"And, since I doubt any of us has yet eaten this morning, would it not be possible to find there bread and ale?"

After a moment, Hopton replied: "Possible."

"And if possible, my friend, might it be probable?" Since the landlord still made no move, he added, "It would, of course, be my honour to pay for same."

Hopton nodded. "Come, then," he said, and led the way across the alley towards his kitchen. None of the three men looked back at the blood, or the knife, or the dead man on the Angel's floor.

"To answer your question, Mr. Woodward," said Pretty, as they ate, "concerning my *particular capacity*. Neither my brother Adam nor I had the honour of being elected to represent our regiment as Agitators. That was what you wished to know, I think? We attended at Putney merely as onlookers."

"Onlookers?" said Hopton. "While the Grandees determined your fate?"

"While the Grandees *discussed* the future of the Kingdom with our Representers," Pretty corrected him. "For as the Romans said, 'That which concerns all ought to be debated by all'."

Hopton snorted, and drank his beer.

"And that being done," said Woodward, "you and your brother were returning to the West, following the ending of the—"

"The ending of all our dreams of liberty," Pretty interrupted. "Following the unconstitutional disbandment of the Army. Following the treachery at Putney. Following the murderous villainy of the new tyrant, Cromwell. Following the —"

"Following the Late Public Differences," said Woodward, firmly. He had been a lawyer for many years, and knew well the force of words. "You paused here at the Angel, to be refreshed from your travels. And whilst here, several men, including Adam, fell into a discussion in Mr. Hopton's backmost room, which in its topics continued that which lately had taken place at Putney. I have that correctly? And you, sir, were also present during these conversations?"

Pretty hesitated before answering. "Yes. I was there."

"And this discussion became . . . heated? Is that so?"

Pretty said nothing.

"Mr. Pretty, may I ask you—and I ask only because I must, you understand—of what Party were you and your brother?"

"Levellers," said Hopton, delivering the word as if it were a mouthful of phlegm.

Woodward ignored him, and looked only at Pretty. "Sir?"

"Your friend has it."

"Thank you, sir. Now, this discussion; how many took part?"

"Five," said Hopton. "This one, his brother, three others."

Woodward swallowed his irritation at the innkeeper's interruptions. "These others, Mr. Pretty. They were known to you?"

Again, Pretty's answer was slow in coming. "Men of the Regiment," he said eventually.

"Fellow soldiers, then. Good. Now Mr. Pretty, I beg you to understand that this matter of Parties is of no import to me. A man's opinions are between him and his God. But to comprehend the death of your brother, I must take note of all insignificant details. You understand? It is my training in the law that makes me this way. These three others—were they of the Leveller persuasion, also?"

Pretty chewed slowly. *Chewing food or thoughts?* Woodward wondered.

"By their words, I took them for supporters of the Presbyterians."

"I see. Well, now, we are all on the same side, are we not?" Woodward looked purposefully at Hopton. "The *victorious* side, by God's grace." Hopton grunted—which was, Woodward supposed, at least better than snorting. "The discussion between you and Adam on one side of the table, and these good Presbyterian gentlemen on the other—it continued for an hour or so?"

Again, the thoughtful pause. *There is something he wants to tell me, but won't,* Woodward thought. *Or something he doesn't want to tell me, but in the end must.*

"The discussion was continuing when I left the room," said Pretty.

"Ah. You left the room?"

"I was weary. I went in search of sleep."

"You had taken a room here at the Angel?"

"I slept in the stable. With the horses."

"Of course—simplicity and modesty in all things. Most commendable." *But sufficient to damn you as a niggard in the innkeeper's eyes,* thought Woodward. "So the first you knew of the tragedy that had befallen your family . . . ?"

"This morning when I awoke, Adam was not alongside me in the stable." Pretty looked at Hopton. "He was upon your floor, Landlord, stabbed to death."

"These three Presbyterian soldiers," said Woodward. "I think it necessary we speak to them now. If they are still to be found."

"In their rooms," said Hopton.

"Still asleep?" said Woodward, a little surprised that parliamentary soldiers of any Party should lay abed so late.

"Asleep or awake, in their rooms is where they'll be." Hopton produced from his sleeve a bunch of keys. "I locked them in, see."

"Through the windows," said Hopton, by way of explanation when he returned some minutes later accompanied by but one Presbyterian soldier. "That's that settled, then, is it not? Clearly, the two who have flown are guilty, and this one who stayed isn't."

The "one who stayed," a solidly-built man of perhaps thirty-five, his head half-bald and his skin walnut-brown, gave his name as William Church, and asked: "What is this talk of guilt? And why was the door to my room locked during the night? Is this an inn or a prison?"

Woodward showed coin to Hopton, which the landlord correctly interpreted as a suggestion that food and drink be fetched for Mr. Church. "Sir, forgive us, I beg of you, these irregularities. Ours is a hospitable town, and I trust you will return to it in happier times, but for now I must tell you that a horrible thing has occurred, and that is that this gentleman's brother has been done to death. Murdered, that is."

Church stared at Pretty. "Murdered? Your gentle brother, that was with us last night?"

"The same one."

Church's heavy eyebrows achieved union, as his face screwed up in thought. "And the two other men that were also present?"

"Gone," said Woodward. "Flown, though it was thought they were caged."

"Flown," said Church, to himself; and then, evidently re-membering his niceties, he added: "Mr. Pretty, I am most sympathetic that you have suffered such a loss as this."

Pretty nodded acknowledgement. Hopton returned with Church's meal, and as the soldier made a somewhat distracted start on it, Woodward told Church his name and profession. "When you have recovered from your shock, sir, I shall ask you to tell me all you know of your two companions from last night, so that I may pass that information to the magistrates."

"Of course," said Church. "Though I knew them but slightly."

"That seems to be the end of the matter," said Hopton.

"It does," said the lawyer, but his tone was uncertain, even if that uncertainty was only noticeable to his own ears. "Tell me something of this Leveller creed of yours, Mr. Pretty, for I would attain a right understanding of it. It's said that you would give all a voice in the choosing of Parliament-men. Is that so?"

"Certainly, sir, for as Colonel Rainborough said at Putney, the poorest he that is in England has a life to live as the greatest he. Meaning that the man who has forty shillings a year has no greater right to representation than has any other free Englishman."

"*Any* Englishman?" said Hopton. "Any man at all, that has a breath and being?"

"Indeed, sir. All men who retain their birthright should be electors, equally."

"It is true what they say, then," said Hopton, horror mingling with disbelief in his voice. "You would destroy all distinctions of degrees between men?"

Through a mouthful of bread, Church said, "More than that, sir. Mr. Pretty and his friends would abolish property itself."

At this, Hopton could only splutter. Even Woodward, who had heard such things said before, felt a little sick. Both men noticed that Pretty did not trouble to deny the accusation.

"Mr. Pretty's belief," Church continued, "is that every man has a *natural right,* given him by God, to choose who shall govern him. Is this not so, sir?"

"It is self-evident, sir," said Pretty.

"Then, sir, you must also say that by the same Law of Nature, which surely states that a man must have sustenance rather than starve, then any man has a right to take my food,

129

my clothes, my house, my crops. He may take what he pleases, for I have only as much natural claim upon those things as he has. And then, sir, we shall be animals, and we shall have anarchy."

Pretty shook his head in obvious irritation. "Not so, sir, for you seem to forget the Law of God, which is above the Law of Nature. The Law of God forbids us theft and murder and adultery. But there is no Law of God that sets one man above another in the matter of who shall govern." He turned to Woodward. "I suppose that men began to choose representatives when there were too many men for all to speak directly. But if we were to start a government today, for the first time, would we say that only the man who has forty shillings a year might have a voice? It is unthinkable!"

Before the lawyer could reply, if such was his intention, Church spoke, his voice urgent. "The granting of an equal voice to every man *must* lead to the ending of property, for how can it not? For the representation of those who have nothing must certainly exceed that of those who have much —"

Pretty struck his fist on the table. "Please God that it should!"

Church's fists tightened, and he took a deep breath before replying. "Yet, that was not your brother's view, Mr. Pretty."

Pretty's face froze. "My brother's view . . . no. Adam argued that, on the contrary, an equitable parliament is the *guarantor* of the rights of property, for it gives to all a material interest in the ease of the Kingdom. If I own a bakery, I might fear the starving man, but I need not fear my neighbour who has a full belly."

"You would do away with *property?*" said Hopton, his face grimacing with perplexity.

The frustrated grinding of Pretty's teeth was audible

around the room. "With this talk of property, we are much deviated from the question, which is only this: may a man be bound by any law that he has not consented to? Nor any of his ancestors, betwixt him and Adam, did ever give consent to. Governance can be by the people's consent alone."

Woodward turned to Church. "But your party of Presbyterians, sir, do not favour this view?"

"That all electors should be equal, yes. But that those equals should be drawn from amongst they that have a *settled* and *permanent* interest in England, which is to say—"

"Which is to say," cried Pretty, half-rising from his chair, "that all men are equal, only some are more equal than others!"

An angry silence fell. Pretty and Church busily avoided looking at each other. Hopton continued to mutter to himself. Woodward sat quietly, deep in troubled thoughts. After a while, he spoke. "Then, gentlemen, I wonder: what is to become of the King?"

"We shall have a king of a new kind, sir," said Church. "A king may be in any form. He can be hereditary or elected, he can enjoy absolute power or limited power—"

"Only superstition makes us desire a king of any shape!" Pretty interrupted.

"Divine law commands us to honour our fathers and mothers, though we have not a choice in who they are," said Church. "This principle can extend."

"But we should honour them only if they are righteous. We have one true King—that is Christ—and we do not need another, except that we do not trust ourselves to govern ourselves. We have been vassals since the Conquest, and now we are ready to regain our freedoms."

"The King is tamed," Church began, but was again interrupted.

"You speak of restoration, but you have not the courage to call it by its name!"

"It is not *restoration,* Mr. Pretty, to say to a man, you had two strong legs, and you used them for kicking the arses of your children, and so from now on your legs will be bound."

"We suffer now under arbitrary government," Pretty shouted. "As the law stands, a king may do what he wishes, soever, and no lawyer or sheriff may call him to account."

"Which is why, sir, if you will only hear me—"

"There can be no compromise with tyranny! I would have you know that I interrupt you with great reluctance, and with only love in my heart," said Pretty, flecks of spit gathering on his lips, "but surely you must see that if the King is restored, then he is our lawful ruler; if he is our lawful ruler, then we have been, these years, in mutinous rebellion against him—"

"To which he will sign an Act of Indemnity."

"How can he, if he be our lawful ruler, sign such an Act? If we are traitors to lawful authority, then we must hang. And, sir—you say the King's legs are to be bound, so that he can no longer kick at the arses of children. I say, if he is king again, then he may order his legs *unbound,* and who can say he must not?"

"Then you say, Mr. Pretty," Woodward asked, "that the King must be tried?"

"*Try* the King?" Hopton gasped.

Church held his head in his hands, as if against a headache. "We cannot put the King on trial, sir, for this very reason—that he is the King! And we are all vowed to—"

"But if a pilot steers his ship towards the rocks," said Pretty, "then the man that takes his command away from him is breaking his vow. Yet who will call such a man a vow-breaker, and not a life-saver? I am not bound to assist that which tends to my own destruction, no matter what engagements I have made."

"It is said by the lawyers—is this not so, Lawyer Woodward?—that a man may not injure himself voluntarily. So that if man enters into a vow—"

"As always, we go around in circles! A vow has no meaning, if the man who made it was not free to refuse it. We have been bereaved of our liberties as Englishmen by the King, and if we do not act we shall be so bereaved by Parliament in its turn, and by the rich men who rule in Parliament. We shall be a nation of pismires."

Both soldiers were standing now, facing each other across the table. Woodward was getting quite a crick in his neck from looking up at them.

"Mr. Pretty," Church said, "in a loving spirit, I would urge you, look at the truth of our situation! The people turn against the Army, because of the demands made upon the realm by this war, because of the famine it has caused—"

"They shall turn against it more, Mr. Church, when they discover that they have been cozened."

"Cozened, you say?" asked Woodward. "How so?"

"For if the King is restored, then we shall have found little fruit of our labours. Do you not think it were a sad and miserable condition, that we have suffered all this time for nothing?"

"For nothing?" Church was so furious, he had taken to pacing. "I shall but humbly take the boldness to put you in mind of one thing: the King is forced to negotiate with us! That is hardly *nothing*."

"Negotiation! With sweetness in my heart for you, sir, and in search only of the justness of the thing, I tell you—the sword alone may sometimes serve for the recovery of stolen rights; you may read that truth in your Bible."

"But what is won by the sword may be lost similarly. If we

allow the King to divide us now, Presbyterian against Independent, he will conquer us. If we dispute, we are lost."

"I cannot agree, sir. God gave us reason that we might use it."

For his part, Woodward thought the Presbyterian had a point. No doubt, Charles would happily side with one Party against the other, for as long as it took to ensure the destruction of both.

"In any case," Pretty continued, "it is too late to talk of not disputing. You know as I do that Cromwell has already begun arresting Levellers. That is what your liberty is worth, sir!"

Enough, thought Woodward; he had seen what he needed to see. He would stop the debate now, before it produced yet more bloodshed. "Gentlemen, your standing and shouting is giving me an inconvenience. I would beg you to sit." Both men—apparently surprised to find themselves standing—obediently sat. "I must ask you both to remain here a little longer. I have the need to perform a small amount of clear thinking, after which I shall return, and then, I believe, the matter of Adam Pretty's death can be settled."

Church frowned. "I had thought that matter already settled, Mr. Woodward?"

"Perhaps, perhaps not. While I am gone, I would suggest that you spend the time in prayer. Mr. Hopton, no doubt, will see to your temporal needs."

"He would abolish *property* and *try* the King," Hopton mumbled, his eyes fixed on, or through, the tabletop.

As Woodward stood to take his leave, Edward Pretty asked him softly: "And you, sir? For what will you pray? Wisdom, or revelation?"

The lawyer smiled. "I fear I am not a greatly prayerful man, Mr. Pretty. It seems safer not to bring myself to God's attention unnecessarily. No, while you gentlemen are at your prayers, I go in search of an onion."

"An onion?"

"For the bowels, sir," said Woodward. "For the bowels. A man must shit well before he may reason well."

"When a thing is done," he told them an hour and a half later, his mind clear now, and his bowels likewise, "it is done for a reason. Or, if not done for a reason, then done out of madness. Either way, it is sense, you will agree, that if we can excavate the *will* behind a particular act, then we shall also expose the actor."

"Thought we'd done so," said Hopton, apparently recovered from his earlier shocks—with the aid of strong drink, if his breath were any guide. "The two flown Presbyterians."

"Ah, yes," said the lawyer. "Five men were debating in your back-most room. As we have seen for ourselves this afternoon, these are dialogues of a kind to bring the flush to a man's cheeks. One man, Edward Pretty, went to bed, leaving four men."

"Not so, sir. I was the first to retire."

"Indeed, Mr. Church? I beg your pardon. I had understood that Mr. Pretty was the first."

"I did not say so," said Pretty.

A successful lawyer's mind is a net, from which little escapes. And Benjamin Woodward was a successful lawyer, if not a wholly successful man. After a moment's recollection, he said: "No more you did, sir. It was I mistook your meaning. So, then; William Church leaves, and four remain. Some time later, Edward Pretty leaves, and three remain."

"And the two," said Hopton, impatiently, "do for the one. We know all this."

"Both of them do for him?"

The landlord waved the question aside. "One of them

does him, and both flee. What does it matter? We have their names, they will be taken eventually."

"Yet why did they not flee upon the instant? Instead, it seems, they murdered poor Adam, then went calmly to bed."

"Perhaps," Church offered, "they acted calm so as to prevent suspicion."

"What, and then escaped through their windows in the morning?"

"They found themselves locked in," Hopton suggested, "thus knew they were discovered, and so fled. This were no mystery."

"Ah, perhaps. But I ask myself also, what was it about poor Adam that drove these men into a killing rage?"

"His many opinions," Hopton insisted. "Concerning the abolition of property."

"Your brother, Mr. Pretty, was a man of strong opinions, strongly spoken?"

"He was as other men," Pretty replied.

"Mr. Church; you found him argumentative?"

"Not overly so."

"No indeed, this I gathered from your remarks earlier. That Adam Pretty held milder views than his brother, and expressed them milder, too." Church looked at Pretty; neither spoke. "An unlikely man, perhaps, to be killed during an argument."

"You believe," said Hopton, "that his killers had some other reason?"

"Possibly. Mr. Church—can you think of any reason?"

Church could. "King's men, seeking to cause disunity within the Army. If those men last night were secretly Royalist agents—"

"Or," said Woodward, gently, "agents of General Cromwell, hunting down Levellers? Mr. Pretty, you say nothing, but surely you would not put such villainy past one who you say is a dictator?"

For a long moment, Pretty stared hard at Church. But when he spoke, it was with a shrug. "I suppose not."

"We have only Mr. Church's own word for his whereabouts at the time of the deed," said Woodward. As Church began to protest, he added: "And the same can be said of Mr. Pretty." Pretty, the lawyer noticed, did not protest. He seemed quite sunk in silent thought. "But in any case, if the murder were plotted, then the plotters made a rough job of it. Though, we must also admit, that if it were done in a moment's madness, then it were done very quietly. Neither Mr. Hopton, nor any of his customers, were alarmed by the noise of an angry struggle. Neither case seems to fit our facts."

"Yet it must have been one or the other," said Hopton. "Either plotting, or ire."

"Yes, my friend, you are right. It was ire of a sort. Was it not, my boy?" He reached across and laid a hand—a consoling, not an arresting, hand—on Edward Pretty's shoulder.

Pretty bowed his head for a moment, and closed his eyes. Then he said: "Of a sort, Lawyer Woodward."

Church fell to his knees. Not in a faint, Woodward decided, but in prayer. Hopton poured ale from a jug, drank it, and did not offer the jug to his guests.

"Before you say more, Edward, I would caution you of this: that I have no proof of anything I have supposed, other than what may come out of your own mouth. No man is obliged to place his own neck in the noose."

"You are a kind man, Mr. Woodward, but I have told you one lie today, and I will not tell you any more. I killed my brother."

Hopton was on his feet. "That is a confession, witnessed by we three. I'll ride to fetch the magistrate. Woodward, you can hold the murderer till morning?"

"He offers no threat to me. Take Mr. Church with you; two will make better time than one."

When Church had been retrieved from his piety, and he and the innkeeper had left, Woodward poured two mugs of beer, and Pretty told his story.

"As you have seen, that man Church and I could not so much as wish each other a good morning without heat entering our words. The other three—well, they talked, too, but with less passion. They tried to turn the conversation to gentler matters, but Church and I were unwilling, or unable, to follow their lead. In the end, it was Church who retired to bed first, as he told you."

"While you, without quite lying, managed to give the impression that you had retired earliest of all."

"I lied only when I said that the discussion continued after I had left. Only one lie, but it is the one for which God shall damn me."

"From the start, I noticed your reluctance to say untruths, and that it caused you to hesitate often in your speech. You are not trained as a lawyer, I suppose?"

"No, sir. I was an ostler, before the—"

"—before the late public—"

"Before the War, Mr. Woodward."

Woodward gave a small, formal bow of concession. "The War, Edward. Quite so. Now, Mr. Church retired . . . ?"

Pretty rubbed at his scalp with his knuckles. "I see now that he did so in order to avoid conflict, that he was guided by God in that action. But at the time, it seemed to me that he offered insult, by withdrawing from a conversation that I was not yet done with."

"You went after him?"

"Not immediately. I stewed for a minute or so. But then, yes, I stood and cried *"Damn the man!"* Forgive me, Mr. Woodward, I am not usually a blasphemer."

"I don't doubt it."

"I stood, and found that my knife was in my hand."

"I do not believe you would have harmed Mr. Church."

Pretty spread his hands. "I trust I should not have. I think I meant only to remonstrate with him. But that is just as wicked! A man who truly loves Christ does not yield to rage, no matter the provocation."

He does after five years of war, thought Woodward, who had learned in his career at law that men returned from fighting were often subject to uncontrollable rages, though they might previously have been of the mildest character.

"I made for the door, and Adam . . . he was my elder and only brother, Mr. Woodward, and sworn to protect me from harm. And had done so, through so many years and across so many miles. And now, only a day from home. . . ."

"Drink had been taken," said Woodward. "You were all perhaps a little unsteady on your feet."

Pretty nodded. "That is how it was. Adam went to take the knife from me, speaking softly, saying *'Quiet now, Brother.'* I made to pass him, but he wouldn't yield. I pushed at him, he held my arm as he fell, and as we landed, the knife entered his belly. He died in my arms. The two Presbyterians, terrified beyond their wits, went white as snow. 'We have seen nothing,' one of them said, and both fled."

"Hopton came upon you like that?"

"He did, some minutes later, puzzled by the silence, perhaps. I told him there had been an accident, which was the truth, and he ordered me to my bed, and to say nothing."

It was not hard for Woodward to imagine Hopton's feelings, for his own might have been similar. *Stay uninvolved and stay alive* had been the motto of many men, throughout those years of tumult. It might be that Hopton truly believed the Presbyterians guilty, and had truly believed that all three were in their rooms when he locked their doors. Or it might be otherwise.

"Why did you not confess your part in the matter? It was an accident, after all. And I see that you loved your brother, and are not a man of criminal character."

"We were closer in love than in beliefs. We had often quarrelled, at Putney. And before. And since. Adam was a true Leveller in the matter of representation, and of the fate of the King, but we differed concerning property."

"Is it such a big difference?"

"Sir, I believe it is all the difference in the world. The difference between bondage deferred, and liberty secured. While some are rich and some poor, none may be free."

"You feared then that some might think you capable of killing Adam in a rage born of debate?"

"That, sir, but even more another thing. You see, I have a mother."

And with that, Woodward felt he understood all. The smallest reason imaginable, in days when every action seemed pregnant with great motives; that a boy could not face the shame of having his mother learn that she had lost one son, by the hand of the other.

The lawyer stood, and gripped the soldier's forearm most urgently. "Ride now, Edward! I will not give you away. To Ireland with you, or France! You cannot put your trust in the Law, we both know that—it is as the song says: *'Rich men in the tavern roar, but poor men pay for all.'* Flee now, in the name of God, and your mother shall have at least one surviving child!"

But Pretty only took the lawyer's hand, and held it firm, and made no move to rise from his chair. "The poorest he must have a voice, and all must be bound equally by the laws of the kingdom. Those are my beliefs. I forgot them, but only for a while. Sit with me, Benjamin Woodward, if you have the time, and we shall wait out the hours together."

In melancholy, Woodward sat, unable to ignore the new and angry knowledge in his heart, that the one man truly responsible for Adam Pretty's death would never pay at all. Whatever fate might befall Charles Stuart, one thing was for certain: England would never find the courage to hang a king. A nation of pismires, indeed.

★ ★ ★ ★ ★

I have no training as a historian. But I can read.

Many British people today, I fear, have not even heard of the English Revolution; most would probably associate the phrase "Civil War" with the United States. (Even then, the version of American history known to the British is very much the same comically inaccurate mixture of propaganda, myth, and misunderstanding which is taught to the Americans themselves by Hollywood and television and other engines of deliberate ignorance.)

And yet the events which serve as a setting for this little story (written in 2000 for Maxim Jakubowski's anthology *Murder Through the Ages*) are of immense importance to anyone who wishes to understand where our modern ideas of democracy, and our forms of government, came from. Obviously, crime fiction can't "teach" history. But it's surely no coincidence that so many writers and readers find a blending of historical research and mystery plotting provides a uniquely satisfying form of literature.

The good news is that, since the invention of the Internet, so much prime historical source material is available to all, free and undistorted. Much of the dialogue in my story is taken directly from contemporary, verbatim accounts of what the speakers said at Putney. Type "The Putney Debates" into a search engine, and see what you come up with; I'm quite certain you'll be as captivated as I was.

TOMORROW'S VILLAIN

For a short while, following the death of my daughter, I became something of a national hero.

It helped that I was an ordinary bloke—a self-employed electrician—and not what the papers call a "toff." The papers hate toffs, which is odd, given that the papers are staffed almost exclusively by toffs.

It helped even more that I was a lone father. Lone mothers are, even these days, still subject to a certain moral ambiguity: is she in that position deliberately? Or did she at least bring it on herself? But a father, struggling bravely against both nature and society to raise a child all on his lonesome—why, he's halfway to being a saint already.

So when Nadine (named for the Chuck Berry song) died in a back street in the West End of London, all I had to do was fight back the tears on live TV and I was instantly canonised.

I made the usual press conference appeal for witnesses, remembering with some guilt as I did so that whenever I'd watched such performances on TV in the past, I'd always assumed that the person making the appeal was the guilty party.

Nadine died one week after her eighteenth birthday, of a rare allergic reaction to the chemicals contained in an anti-rape spray. Normally, so the coroner later declared, this would not have led to a fatality; however, there was evidence at the death scene of a scuffle, during which, it was surmised, her assailant had held the canister close to her face and emptied its entire contents directly into her mouth and nose. Her death, essentially from respiratory failure, had followed rapidly. I was astonished to learn that Nadine carried such a spray —she loathed all weapons —but I supposed that no parent ever knows their children as well as they think they do.

Within seventy-two hours of my daughter's death, the police made an arrest: a 21-year-old, black, male shop assistant, Horace Jones. The next day's papers described him variously as Nadine's "live-in lover" and "steady boyfriend." I'd never heard of him.

A black, male killer, a white, female victim; a brave but grief-stricken dad. We were news, the three of us.

These events happened in November, so they were still fresh in the public's mind when a national radio station ran its annual "Man of the Year" phone-in poll. I won. That made me laugh. I mean, *really* laugh—laugh with real amusement. I was the Man of the Year for having lost my daughter. If I'd had two daughters, and they'd both been killed, would I have been elected Pope?

Horace Jones denied all charges, both at the time of his arrest, and a few months later, during his trial. His denials were not believed, and he was duly sentenced to life imprisonment.

His trial put me back in the headlines, and my heroic status was confirmed and even enlarged. I really believe that, at that moment, I could have stood for Parliament with some hope of success. Nadine was a victim, Horace Jones was emblematic of all that was wrong with modern Britain, and I was . . . well, I seemed to be, for no reason that was ever clear to me, the symbol of all that was *right* with modern Britain.

Jones' lawyer lodged an appeal against the conviction. As it happened, I knew the lawyer, Teddy Edwards, had known able, but wrong: in fact, I had taken in, and retained, every word of that trial. As long as the trial went on, Nadine still existed. People still spoke of her, and what does being alive mean other than being talked about? "As I recall, there were two main pieces of physical evidence. First of all, the wounds to your client's face . . ."

"Right," said Teddy. "The nail scratches. The wounds were the right age, and they came from a woman's hand, or to be precise from false nails—fun nails, they're called these days. We didn't contest that, but remember that the prosecution was unable to say that they came from *Nadine's* nails. And that's not just a technicality, Jack."

"The wounds were said to be made by a woman of adine's height."

He shrugged. "She was of average female height. Means thing."

"All right. What about the fingerprints?"

"The clincher, as far as the jury was concerned," Teddy itted. "Horace's prints were on the canister of anti-rape y. Nobody else's, not even Nadine's. He says, as you'll mber, that he and Nadine had met in a pub in Covent en a month before her death, right?"

nd that they'd seen each other 'as friends only' several during that month. Yes, I remember." So much for the reports that she'd been killed by her "Black Live-In" "But when your barrister asked him in court if, that time, he had handled the spray can, he couldn't ld he?"

couldn't say," said Teddy. "Wouldn't say. And that's Jack. You know that barristers never ask questions 't already know the answer to?"

heard it said."

we thought we knew the answer to that one. We

him, at least, some years earlier, when we'd served together on a local anti-apartheid committee here in Maidstone. About a week after Jones began his sentence, Teddy phoned and asked to see me. I agreed; I was still in that stage of grief where I wanted more details, more information, more understanding of what had happened.

"He's not guilty, Jack," Teddy said as we sat drinking tea in my empty kitchen. "I'm sorry, I know that probably isn't what you want to hear, but I have to tell you: I have no doubt in my mind at all that Horace Jones did not kill Nadine."

It wasn't what I wanted to hear, of course, and it wasn't what I'd expected to hear. "You have to say that, don't you, Teddy?" I replied. "A lawyer—you've got to believe your clients are innocent. That's how it works, surely?"

He shook his head. "Not at all, Jack. Not like that at all. Ninety-nine per cent of my clients are thieves and liars and worse. I have to *accept* that they're innocent if that's what they choose to tell me, but I'm not required to *believe* it. I represent them to the best of my ability, because that's my job— and because," and here he paused for a self-deprecating chuckle, "and because, now that I'm a middle-aged, middle-class solicitor, I actually do believe in the system. I'm not the radical I once was, Jack. Well, which of us is? I think our system of law is, overall, a good system. And it can only work as long as even the most heinously guilty arsehole gets the best defence the system can provide him with. But no, I don't usually believe their pathetic fairy stories."

"So what's different this time?" I asked.

He sat forward in his seat, and started ticking off items on his fingers. "OK. Right. Basically, I think Horace has been lynched. He's black, Nadine was white. She was a lovely girl training to be a nurse; he's just some inner-city nobody with a petty criminal record: possession of drugs, some minor thieving. It's a match made in Hell."

"Just because ignorant people wanted him to be guilty doesn't mean he *wasn't* guilty," I said.

"No, sure, good point." Teddy looked tired and sweaty. He'd aged a lot in the few years since I'd last seen him. Much of his hair had gone, and his suit was irreversibly rumpled. It was a reasonably expensive suit, so I assumed the rumpling came from within. He took a packet of cigarettes out of his pocket and waved it at me. "Do you mind if I smoke?"

"No, of course not."

"Really," said Teddy, "say if you do."

I shook my head, and stood up to find him an ashtray. "Nadine smoked."

"They all do, don't they?" he said, lighting up gratefully. "Teenage girls. My wife says the ones you want to worry about are the ones who don't smoke. You can guarantee they're doing something much worse."

Teddy went back to talking about the case, putting forward his arguments concerning Horace Jones's innocence, but after a while he noticed that I wasn't hearing him.

"Christ, Jack, are you all right?"

It was the smell of the cigarette. Before Teddy, the last person who'd smoked in that house had been Nadine. For some reason, when everyone came back here for the funeral meats, all the smokers were careful to take their cigarettes out into the garden, even though there were ashtrays on every surface in the kitchen and living room. A kind of bizarre, turn-of-the-century mark of respect for the dead: don't let them see you smoking.

When the snake of aromatic grey and white smoke from Teddy's cigarette coiled across the table between us and up into my brain, I instantly and absolutely broke down. From a man of flesh, holding things together, I turned into a bowl of

dry cornflakes: shattered, jagged, formless. And then soggy, as the tears flowed. I wasn't sobbing: I was just sitting there staring straight ahead, while the tear-water poured out of my eyes like beer from a tap.

Teddy helped me through to the living room. He drew curtains, put the lights on, poured us both a scotch from almost full bottle on the sideboard. I'd hardly been i living room since Nadine died. I felt out of place, almos itor in my own home, and I think that helped me rega trol of my tear ducts.

After a while, I was ready to resume the conv Teddy wasn't smoking any more.

"I don't know how much of the trial you took don't imagine legal niceties were uppermost in but let me tell you—and you don't have to take it, I'll get you a transcript of the trial—there wa evidence against Horace. No serious evidence.

"Then how did he get convicted?" I asked. now you believed in our system of law."

"Yeah, sure, but compared to *what*—that' Teddy rubbed his hands over his scalp, mak he had left stand up in tufts. He looked like woken up grumpy from an afternoon nap, thing is either perfect or terrible. But a r context. All I'm saying is, if you were an no money, charged with a terrible crim rather be tried: Britain or America? Bri or Spain?"

"But this time the system got it wr telling me?"

"I'm sure of it."

"OK," I said, the details of th coming back to me. Teddy's ass

thought Horace was going to reply that Nadine had spilt her handbag once when they were out together, and that he had helped her re-pack it. Hence the single set of his prints on the spray."

"So why didn't he?"

Teddy shook his head. "Don't know. Actually, yes, I think I do—because it was a lie. I don't think that is how his prints got on there, and he is the kind of bloke—something of an innocent, religious upbringing—that he's just not willing to tell a lie. Even to save his neck."

Now I shook my head—the scotch was clouding my mind a little. I hadn't had a drink since the day of the funeral. "But if even you think he's lying about the anti-rape spray . . ."

"My guess is that he knows something about what happened, but he's not willing to say it. So, to avoid lying, he just says nothing. Or else, *I don't know, Sir,* which amounts to the same thing." Teddy stood up. "Look, Jack, I'm sorry. I've given you a bad evening. I'll let you get some kip, now. But can I talk to you again? I really think it's important."

"Of course you can," I said. "I'm always happy to talk." *About Nadine,* I didn't need to add.

Teddy sent me the trial transcript, and I read it, feeling a jet of life squirt up through my body every time I saw the word *Nadine* in print.

The prosecution's case was straightforward. Horace and Nadine first met in a pub in Covent Garden. They went out together several times over the next few weeks, to pubs, clubs, ethnic restaurants. They did not sleep together. They chatted about the things they had in common: football (she was a West Ham fanatic, my daughter), exotic food and 1960s rhythm and blues music.

On the night of her death, they had been drinking in a pub

off the Charing Cross Road. At closing time, they walked towards Leicester Square Tube station, taking a short cut through an unlit alley. There, Horace demanded sex. Nadine refused. Horace persisted, to the point of attempted rape (her clothes were in disarray when she was found). She tried to use the anti-rape spray on him, but he took it from her and turned it on her, forcing it into her mouth and nose. When he saw the effect this had on her, he panicked and ran. She was found dead by an off-duty ambulance driver about forty minutes later. At around that time, a blood-splashed black youth was seen running in a nearby street.

Horace Jones was a suspect from the start of the investigation, according to the prosecution's version of events. Detectives learned of his existence from some girls at Nadine's college, and heard from the same source that he and Nadine had been seen "arguing violently" in a Covent Garden wine bar the night before her death. He was described as "a big, strong man" which caught the detectives' attention, since it had already been noted that the method of death probably ruled out a female killer, a short man, or a weakling.

When taken in for questioning, Horace denied killing Nadine, or fighting with her, or attempting to rape her, but he declined to give an account of his movements during the crucial hours. He also refused to explain the scratches on his face, and when, on the second day of questioning, he was confronted with the fingerprint evidence, he offered no comment. At the end of the second day, he was charged with murder.

The police did everything by the book: no doubt about that. It's clear from the interview transcripts that they went to great lengths to persuade Horace that he ought to be represented by a lawyer—"Don't need a lawyer, man. I got no lies to tell"—and the interviews were interrupted repeatedly for tea breaks, and on three further occasions so that Horace could be seen by the duty surgeon, "as the prisoner appeared to be in a state of considerable emotional shock."

They'd got their man, and they weren't going to lose him through a procedural error. Or else maybe they were just good cops, trying to do the job properly. I suppose that's not impossible, after all.

"Have you read it?" said Teddy on the phone.

"I have."

"Great. Thanks. Listen, sorry to have to, you know, put you through—"

"That's OK. Don't worry."

"OK, great." A pause, during which I wondered whether there were any cigarettes in Nadine's room. I'd never smoked, not even as a kid, but it would be nice to smell that scent again. "Listen, Jack—I'd like you to meet him. Horace: I'd like you to talk to him."

I almost dropped the phone, as my heart stopped pumping and my limbs froze. *Meet him?* "Is that . . . would that be allowed?"

"Oh yeah, yeah, listen—yeah." Teddy was gabbling. In gratitude, I suppose, that I wasn't screaming at him. "I mean, you know, a prisoner's allowed visitors. Up to him who they are."

"And he's willing?"

Teddy laughed. "About as willing as you are, Jack! But, yes, he'll see us. If you think you're up to it."

How much easier it must have been in the days of capital punishment, I thought. *At least back then the ghosts were all dead.*

"So you've read the evidence, what do you think?" We were in Teddy's car, driving to the prison. "There's not much to it, is there?"

"I agree it's a bit thin," I said. "But if Horace didn't do it, and he wasn't there, then why wasn't he able to offer a more convincing defence? Some sort of alibi, or something."

"I'm hoping," said Teddy, who seemed a lot more nervous than I was, "that we'll find that out today."

I, by contrast, was not hoping for anything in particular. Why was I there? The usual reason: to prolong the existence of Nadine.

"You won't get a word out of our Horace," said the prison officer who checked our papers. "He's the tall, dark, silent type." When the guard clocked my name, he gave me a look that only just fell short of naked contempt. That was an omen, if I'd been in a state to notice it. But all such thoughts fled my head the moment I sat down opposite Horace and looked into his eyes for the first time.

I knew straight away that he hadn't killed my daughter.

It wasn't anything to do with him. It wasn't that I looked upon Horace and knew him incapable of murder. It was rather that I looked at Horace and knew *Nadine* to have been incapable of being murdered by him.

Nonsense, of course. Irrational, meaningless. I understood that then no less than I understand it now, but that understanding didn't change what I knew. One thing that having your daughter murdered does for you—did for me, at any rate—is it liberates you from the rules of rationality. If you know something, you just know it, and you don't ask how or why. I had already accepted the utterly impossible fact that my only child had predeceased me; after that, accepting any lesser impossibility was child's play.

Teddy introduced us—as if we needed it!—and then sat with his chair slightly behind mine, leaving the two of us alone in a room full of chattering, grieving men and women.

"All right, Horace," I said, without preamble. "You didn't kill Nadine. So who did?"

Horace said nothing, just stared at me with the eyes of a disinterred corpse. He didn't blink, and he didn't look away.

"Do you think your need not to tell is greater than my need to be told? Is that it, Horace? Because if so, then there's nothing I can—"

He blinked. Once. It was one of the most effective interruptions I have ever been subjected to. I stopped talking, and waited.

At last, he said: "I don't want to tell you. Being in here is better than telling it. It's terrible in here, but it's better than telling it." But he did tell us his story, even so. Not all of it—not even then—but enough.

A week later, Teddy and I held a press conference. Teddy gave a broad outline of the case for an appeal hearing, while I answered follow-up questions from the reporters—all of which were of the idiotic "How do you feel?" variety. My well-rehearsed answer was simple: I felt it was wrong that a man should be in prison for a crime he hadn't committed. I felt that those actually responsible for my daughter's death should be brought to justice. Beyond that, I had no comment to make.

The Campaign for Justice for Horace Jones was formally launched, with Teddy as its Treasurer and me as its Secretary—and thus, within the space of a day, I passed from being yesterday's hero to being tomorrow's villain.

To the newspapers, I was no longer an ordinary working bloke; I was a "self-employed businessman." I was no longer a brave lone father, struggling to raise his beautiful daughter; I was now a "divorcee loner," who had raised a "wild child." (The fact that my ex-wife had died in a motor accident shortly before our divorce had been finalized, and that I was therefore technically a widower, went unmentioned.)

I was, above all, no longer that quiet, unassuming dad who bore his bereavement with solemn dignity. Now, I was that crazy do-gooder who wanted to let a murdering monster out of jail to kill again. (A *black* monster. The word was always there, even though it rarely appeared in print.)

One journalist—who I later discovered was all of twenty-two years old, fresh down from Oxford, and a niece by marriage of the proprietor—wrote an op-ed piece in the *Daily Telegraph*, telling the world (and, incidentally, me) precisely what it was that I was doing, and why. The *what* was putting my "white liberal conscience" and "knee-jerk pro-ethnic bias" before the "natural love a proper father feels for his child." And the reason I was doing this was, as far as I could make out, because that was what white liberals did.

It was all a case of "political correctness gone mad," the writer concluded (demonstrating that what she lacked in empathy she made up for in cliché-mongering), and furthermore it was this "false prioritisation, born of middle-class guilt and enforced by the liberal theocracy," that had led to the breakdown of family-based, Christian society. And so on: I'm sure you're familiar with the script.

Daft, I know, but it was that word "liberal" that annoyed me most. I have never been *remotely* liberal; I am a socialist son of socialist parents. My daughter was a socialist. My great-grandfather was arrested seven times during the General Strike. If Lucinda Buckteeth-Jodhpurs, or whatever the silly little bitch's name was, wanted to get into a liberal-despising contest with me, she'd better be prepared for a heavy defeat. My wife, now, she *was* a liberal. Probably one of the reasons we split up—I don't mean because we argued about politics, but because, being a liberal, she had no moral impediment to abandoning her husband and child to pursue self-fulfilment.

Smart comedians, bored with their usual diet of bent politicians and ugly TV celebrities, made neat little gags at my expense. They couldn't be accused of racism, of course, because they were being *ironic*.

It wasn't only the mass media that took an interest in me. Someone painted "Wog Lover" in large, ironically black letters on my garage door. Of the two attackers, I found I had more respect for the spray-painter than for the *Telegraph* girl. They were both saying the same thing, after all—*exactly* the same thing, make no mistake about that—but at least the painter didn't try to disguise himself with the false-beard-and-moustache of education, privilege, and logorrhea.

I left the legend on the garage door, didn't try to clean it off. I decided instead to treat it as a compliment. "Wog Lover?" Sure, why not? I *do* try to love my neighbour: that's how I was brought up. It's how my daughter was brought up.

Besides, if I'd cleaned it off, someone would only have put it back, wouldn't they? I could have been out there with a bucket and scrubbing brush every day for the rest of my life.

There was much more in a similar vein, but it's not worth listing. No one actually hit me or put a bomb through my window. As for the rest—well, if you want the truth, being a national villain was considerably less irritating than being a national hero had been. At least I could get my car out of my garage without first clearing several dozen bouquets of damn lilies away from the door.

"I'm really sorry," Teddy said one night over a beer, in my living room. The campaign to secure an appeal hearing went on for two years—a much quicker process than it had been in the recent past, Teddy was always at pains to point out. In America they bury their mistakes, he'd say. At least Horace is still alive.

155

"You're sorry for what?" I asked, though I knew what he meant.

"All this. If I'd known it was going to be so hard on you—"

"You'd have done it anyway," I said, putting an end to the discussion. Because he *would* have done it anyway, and he'd have been right to do it, so what was the point of pretending otherwise?

The appeal hearing revealed the usual tragic, tawdry story of errors and evasions. It wasn't so much a case of evidence being deliberately hidden in order to frame the innocent—more a case of facts which didn't fit being ignored, so as not to ruin a good theory. Evidence, for instance, suggesting that there had been more than two people involved in the scuffle which led to Nadine's death. Evidence which showed that Nadine's death might have been caused by one strong man, *or* by a number of smaller, weaker people acting together.

Everyone does that, don't they? Leaves out the bits that don't fit. Cops do it, politicians do it, school teachers, scientists, sports commentators.

In the dock, this time, Horace told the story that he had told me when I visited him in prison.

"Nadine and me, we were friends, OK? Nothing more. I don't care if you all believe that or not, that's the truth. That is the *truth*. I'm not gay or nothing, but she already had a boyfriend. She was seeing a married man."

That was the bit he hadn't wanted me to hear, because of what had happened between me and Nadine's mother. He was right: I didn't want to hear it. I didn't want to hear evidence, in a court of law, that I had raised a daughter who was merely human, not perfect.

"The night she died, the night they killed her, she and I

had a drink, and then she went to meet this fellow, John."

Don't call her She, I wanted to say. *If you call her Nadine she still exists.*

"He was supposed to be at a meeting in Birmingham, but he wasn't, he was meeting her at a hotel in Hampstead. But when we split up after our drink, and she was going to one Tube and I was going to another, I followed her. I decided to follow her, because . . ."

During a long pause, no one in the court tried to prompt him.

". . . I wasn't her boyfriend, OK? Whatever everybody thinks. I just followed her because I was—because I decided to follow her to see if, you know. Just to *see.* When she turned into that alley, near the Tube, I saw that I wasn't the only one following her. There was four girls, four young women, and they were following her too. I saw them. They had this can of spray, I didn't know what it was then, just a can of something. The main girl, the leader, she was wearing gloves. I saw what they did, and I ran up to them and I was shouting at them to stop and I tried to grab the can, but one of the girls, she raked my face with those long nails. I couldn't see too good, there was blood all in my eyes, and I . . . I ran off to get help. To get some help, you see? For Nadine."

That was the bit he hadn't wanted *anyone* to hear. That was why he had gone to prison for a crime he hadn't committed: to avoid telling the world that he had run from four girls.

"I don't think they meant to kill her. I think they just meant to beat her up. But she . . . Nadine collapsed when they sprayed that stuff in her face." Another long, uninterrupted pause. "I ran off to get help."

A young black man—a young black *male,* as the newspapers always say—running through the streets of the West

End, blood running down his face, shouting about murder. He couldn't find a policeman, and no citizen was brave enough to help him. Are you surprised?

By the time he got back to the scene, Nadine was dead.

"I went home," Horace concluded. He was asked by the Crown's barrister and by his own why he had simply gone home, why he hadn't stayed with the body, called the police, called an ambulance? I don't know why they asked: surely the answer was obvious. The poor kid was ashamed.

Horace Jones did not receive a proper pardon, but he was released on a technicality. He went to live, Teddy told me, with a distant relative somewhere in the Midlands. He changed his name. He refused to sell his story to the newspapers, which means that if the reporters ever do catch up with him they'll consider it their solemn duty to rip his life to shreds. I only hope that by then he's got a life worth ripping.

I never saw him again, except for briefly in Teddy's office, immediately after his release, when I just had time to ask him one question.

"People saw you and Nadine arguing the evening before she died. What were you arguing about?"

He gave me that dead stare. I didn't know if he was going to answer, until he spoke. "Football," he said.

"Football?"

"I don't like football. I like cricket. In cricket you get fair play."

I've no idea if that was the truth. Could have been, I suppose. Funny thing is, Nadine and I used to have that same argument. I'm a cricket man, myself.

On the steps of the appeal court, a police spokesman announced that "As far as we are concerned the case remains closed"—police code for, "Of course the bastard was guilty—

we wouldn't have arrested him otherwise, would we?" But they were humiliatingly forced to abandon this position only a few days later, when one of the girls involved in the attack on Nadine broke ranks, and turned herself in at her local police station, accompanied by her family lawyer.

She hadn't been directly involved in the violence, she said. Leading the attack had been her best friend, the wife of the man Nadine was seeing, along with the wife's two sisters. They'd set out to teach Nadine to "keep her filthy hands off other women's blokes" but "it had all gone horribly wrong" and she could "no longer live with the guilt."

She was charged with a lesser offence; the other three were charged with murder. Their case is due to be heard early next year. And I, naturally, am a public hero once again. I am the courageous, loving father who fought for an innocent boy's freedom against the forces of bigotry and ignorance. My drive is full of bouquets again. I hate it. I'm thinking of moving, changing my name, going abroad. But I'm afraid that to do so would be to surrender to cynicism, and I am determined not to do that. Cynicism is the triumph of death and futility, and I won't willingly become its ally.

Of course, to some I am still a "Wog Lover," and poor Horace is still a murdering savage who got away with it. A Conservative MP, hiding behind the parliamentary privilege of immunity to the laws of slander, told the House of Commons that in his opinion the police had acted correctly throughout, only to have their actions "second-guessed by subversives," and that Horace Jones was "a guilty, guilty man with a soul as black as tar."

To my astonished delight, the MP's party leadership disowned him, his local activists turned against him, and his career fell into a terminal decline. So, then: there *are* still good people in the world. Perhaps I'm even one of them, since the campaign to free Horace began, for me, as a means of keeping Nadine's name alive—but somewhere along the way it became something else: a desire to prove that in a world full of shrugged shoulders, it is still possible to give witness to the simple, concrete difference between right and wrong.

I try to remember that, I mine that thought for whatever comfort it contains, now that the whole business is over and done with, now that my daughter Nadine finally does not exist, and can never exist again.

★ ★ ★ ★ ★

For centuries, people have dreamt of achieving freedom of the press. It remains a dream: for the most part, all over the world, newspapers are controlled either by the government or by wealthy proprietors. One of the nastiest traits of papers in the latter category is their habit of deciding, more or less at random, to turn private individuals into public heroes or villains—and then back again, as the mood takes them.

I wanted to write about that; I also wanted to write a story about decent people trying to behave decently, which after all, is what most of us are most of the time. On the whole, it's the evildoers who make a story exciting—but now and then, you've got to give the majority a look-in, even in crime fiction.

This story first appeared in *Shots*, in 1999.

BITS

Many things led to the killing of Ian Unwin, but the beginning was when Tony Shaw's leather jacket was stolen in a pub near King's Cross. He'd stupidly left it unattended for about two minutes, while he crossed the uncrowded lounge bar to buy some cigarettes from a machine by the Gents. When he got back his jacket had gone, and with it his wallet, chequebook, cheque guarantee card, ATM card, credit cards, union membership card—the lot, the whole pack.

Tony made all the right phone calls, cancelled everything, and so was very annoyed when his next current account statement showed that several of the missing cheques had been used.

He left the town hall half an hour early that afternoon, and asked to see the manager at his local bank. After a longish wait, a woman—a girl really, she looked about twelve—appeared from behind a mirror-glassed door, wearing an expression which hovered between irritation and nervousness.

"Can I help you, please?"

"Are you the manager?"

"I'm your Personal Branch Banker," said the girl, her intonation suggesting that the words held no individual meaning for her.

Tony, wondering how she could be his Personal Branch Banker when she hadn't even asked his name yet, explained about the cheques which had been cashed after he'd reported them stolen.

161

His Personal Branch Banker took down his details, including home and work phone numbers, and then spent ten minutes fiddling at a computer which she had obviously not been trained to use. Eventually she must have elicited an answer of some sort, for she turned back to Tony and said, "Mr. Shaw, is it?"

Tony said it still was.

"Um—actually, Mr. Shaw, are you aware that your account currently shows an unauthorised negative balance of nine hundred pounds?"

"Oh, for Christ's sake," he groaned, and began explaining it all again.

A week later he'd heard nothing, and so flexitimed another half-hour for a return match. The Personal Branch Banker had changed sex, was now a twelve-year-old boy, and had never heard of Mr. Shaw or his fugitive checks. Once more, Tony went through the story, but it wasn't until six weeks, eleven letters and seven phone calls to head office later that the stain on his account was expunged. The penultimate conversation included the following exchange:

Senior Account Supervisor (London): Mr. Shaw, the cheques in question appear to bear the signature 'D. Duck.' Is that your normal form of signature, can you confirm?

Tony: My normal form of signature is 'A. L. Shaw.'

Senior Account Supervisor (London): Ah, right. OK, yeah.

Over the next few months, Tony thought about The Donald Duck Business quite a lot. Thinking about things quite a lot was one of the things he did most. He enjoyed thinking, sorting, planning, puzzling things out. He lived alone, had no noticeable family, either immediate or extended, and one of the reasons he liked living alone was so that he had time to think about things.

He made a list, indexed it on his List of Lists, and filed it in his List Box. The list said:

1. Seeing the manager was a waste of time. No one sees their bank manager these days—indeed, don't even have managers to see.

2. Everything is computers these days. Nobody actually knows anyone. Not like when I was a kid.

3. I have never met my landlord, Mr. Chipping. I met his agent once, when I moved in, and all dealings since have been by post or by messages on answering machines.

4. I have never actually met most of the people with whom I am in regular contact at work. They work in different buildings, in different parts of the borough, and even many of those in the same building communicate by phone, fax, or internal mail.

5. Although I am only forty, the world I inhabit now is already a different planet to the one I was born on. What will it be like when I am sixty?

6. The world today exists in bits. The old cow was right when she said "There is no such thing as society." Modern urban life for the upper-working/lower-middle class (i.e., most of us) is fragmented, automated, alienated.

7. From what I have heard, it is worse in the suburbs. Here in West Hampstead, people do at least occasionally say "hi" to each other, in passing. Out in Metroland, apparently, nobody knows their neighbours, nobody talks to anybody, nobody notices anything—or if they do notice, they don't give a toss.

He named the file "Bits." He found what it told him of life

faintly shocking, rather sad in a generalised way, but not personally discomfiting. Tony had given up on life—on LIFE, anyway—long ago; not out of bitterness or depression or frustration, but just because he had discovered that his wants and ambitions were modest ones.

He would be quite happy—really, perfectly content—to spend the rest of his days sitting in a comfortable armchair, with a book, a glass of whisky, a cigarette, and the knowledge that he would always have somewhere warm to sleep.

Not that Tony was a hermit. He lived a fairly solitary life, true, but he didn't actively shun other people—he just wasn't addicted to them. He preferred human company to be rationed, on his terms. Most of the time he was happy at home, listening to blues on his CD, watching the telly, or reading (SF or fantasy mostly, but only the good stuff). Once a week, however—or more, he was no slave to routine—he would visit a pub. There were several decent ones in walking distance.

And once or twice a year, in one of these casually cheerful places, he would get off with a woman. The last few had been, he readily acknowledged to himself, just a bit on the ropy side. He was no great catch, after all—an ordinary bloke, ordinary looking—and though at one time he had been able to impress young girls with his quiet, worldly maturity, he found that the present young generation had little interest in sex. They all worked in banks.

Never mind: he got by. He wasn't a superstud, and he wasn't celibate. He was fine, he got by.

Tony had no close friends, as such; had never seen the need for them. Instead, he had drinking companions—not rowdy, big boozers, more like playing-the-quiz-machine, doing-the-crossword-in-the-evening-paper, moaning-about-the-Tube companions. The sort of people who drift in and out of the margins of each other's lives, and only notice that one of their number isn't around any more during nostalgically drunken evenings of "Whatever happened to old whatsisname . . . ?"

Work didn't come into it. He'd been in the same department since leaving school at fifteen, so his salary and conditions of service were quite acceptable. He didn't mind the job particularly, it wasn't hard or dangerous or painfully boring, but he was always glad to get away from it. And he did have a dream.

Tony Shaw dreamed of ER/VR: Early Retirement/Voluntary Redundancy. As municipal government throughout the nation disintegrated, Tony dreamed of his fiftieth birthday, when his eternally cost-cutting employers would gratefully relieve him and themselves of the burden of his employment. At fifty, he would be free, with a pension and a small lump sum, and a reasonable expectation of enough remaining years in which to enjoy them. Quietly; securely.

Even then, though, at the back of his mind, was a sharp splinter of perfect self-knowledge: in common, he imagined, with many people whose ambitions were small, his ruthlessness in pursuing them could be, if necessary, unlimited. After all, he didn't ask for much—he was surely entitled to the little he did ask for?

Tony found that thought comforting; then, and later.

Five years after The Donald Duck Business, something terrible happened to Tony's plans. The council announced that the current round of ER/VR would be the last. Management had decided that their staff reduction exercises had reached a point where the cost of further redundancies would be greater than the cost of maintaining existing staffing levels.

Tony was still only forty-five. There was no way he could

escape now. And, according to the memo he read and re-read, no way he could escape *ever*.

There had to be! That was all, there just had to be. One thing was certain; he couldn't carry on spending eight hours a day away from his chair, his book, his whisky, five days a week, forty-six weeks a year, for the next twenty years!

Impossible. He'd been dreaming of early retirement for almost half his working life. If the realisation of his dream, his modest dream, was not to be given to him, then he would have to find a way to take it.

He'd have to, that's all.

Almost wild with anger—in a rare, scorching rage—Tony Shaw literally ran from his office. It wasn't quite half-ten in the morning, but he didn't tell anyone where he was going, he didn't leave any messages, he didn't open the rest of his post or switch off his terminal. He just ran: to the lift, out of the door, down the street, into the Underground.

And when he stopped running, he was in a pub near Hampstead station.

He was, at least, in sufficient command of his senses to have come to this pub, and not to the one he preferred, further up the hill, but which he had had to abandon a few weeks earlier. That was the pub where Michelle drank.

She probably wouldn't be there so early in the day, but he couldn't take the risk. Michelle had become a real nuisance, a one-night stand that had turned into something perilously close to "a relationship." That was what she called it; that was what she wanted.

Tony was always honest with his women. He never pretended to be looking for love, never pretended to be interested in anything but a brief interlude of mutually refreshing sex. It wasn't his fault, then, that Michelle had failed to understand the rules of engagement—or of non-engagement.

She was a good bit younger than him (mid-thirties, he guessed, though she didn't say, and he never asked) and considerably better-looking than he'd lately been used to. Tony had enjoyed being with her, once, even twice, but somehow she'd got it into her head that they were a couple. Michelle's skin was thick as well as pretty, and no amount of straight talking rid her of her troublesome illusions. When Tony would gently but firmly explain that, sorry, he didn't feel the same way about her as she apparently felt about him, she'd just smile and say, "That's OK. I know how hard men find it to talk about their emotions. It's your upbringing."

Thus it was that Tony now sat in a pub he didn't much care for, trying to find a way round a problem which was even more threatening than the Michelle situation.

It didn't take him long. All he had to do, after all, was give his subconscious a bit of a stir, and then decide if he could stomach what came to the surface.

Halfway though his second pint, he decided he could.

Which meant that he had lists to see to: to begin with, one to steal and one to make.

The stolen list—the details of all those who had been accepted for the current, final round of ER/VR—was not hard to come by. In fact, he didn't even have to leave his office; just press a few keys on his computer, and make an educated guess or two.

When the system had been installed, the computer company woman who trained the council staff in its use had told everybody the same thing: "Give yourself a password that isn't easy to guess, something random. Not your name, for instance." But she had taken a shine to Tony, who was a good pupil, and had added to him, confidentially, "Six months from now, ninety-five per cent of the passwords in this building will be user's names. It's always the same—people forget their original term, and end up thinking *What the hell, there's nothing confidential here, anyway.* You see if I'm not right."

She was right.

Back home, a printout of the stolen list safely in his pocket, Tony made another list. He headed it OPERATION POD, in honour of one of his all-time favourite SF films:

1. Male, obviously.

2. Roughly same age (few years either side might not matter).

3. Good deal—big pension and lump sum—so, long service.

4. Home owner, preferably paid off mortgage.

5. No visible family.

6. Suburban address.

7. Good sick record, so not visiting doctor etc. often enough to be known.

Comparing the two lists quickly eliminated most of the retirees, but left six possibles; six potential hosts, as Tony thought of them.

The next stage of selection required some footslogging, not just paper shuffling.

In truth, Ian Unwin looked good to Tony right from the start, but he nonetheless worked methodically through his shortlist, with the aid, naturally, of another list of criteria:

1. Physical appearance: similar, or easily adapted to (i.e., long hair doesn't matter, but baldness is no good; slight weight gain or loss would be feasible, but

height must be close).

2. Position of house (definitely not flat or maison-ette, bungalow best of all). As few neighbours as possible.

3. *Must have garden*—must not be overlooked by neighbours' windows.

4. Host's routine, weekends, evenings etc: make sure, as far as possible, no regular visitors (including lovers, relatives), and no regular outings—hobbies, groups, church etc.

All this took time; he could have spent forever on it, of course, checking and double-checking, being ultra-cautious. But he didn't have forever. As it was, Tony used up his remaining fortnight of annual leave watching and eliminating. And in the end, as he had suspected at the beginning, it was Ian Unwin who passed all the tests most satisfactorily.

The clincher came on his third secret visit to the Ruislip cul-de-sac, bordering a park, in which Ian lived. Ian's only next-door neighbour had had a For Sale sign in the garden on Tony's first visit. That sign now read "Sold."

"Well then, Ian," said Tony to the silent street. "You're it."

Tony handed in his notice at work—having now, he explained to his boss, given up all hope of ever securing a decent ER/VR deal.

Sonia, the friendly, overworked, young woman who had been his supervisor for the last eighteen months, was only too pleased to give him the reference he asked for, and to make it one that glowed like the sun above. A quiet guy, not very matey, but that was his business. He was always pleasant enough, and everyone knew he was a good worker.

"Got something lined up, Tony?" she asked, having made

the appropriate noises about how much he'd be missed.

"Well, you know," he said. "Fingers crossed."

"Local government?"

He made a wry face. "No thanks! A book shop, as it happens. Old schoolmate, looking for a manager. While *he* takes early retirement, if you're into irony."

She smiled. "A book shop, how lovely! I quite envy you. Local?"

"No. Nottingham, in fact. Cheap property, clean air. Good beer. I fancied a real change." He grinned; he could quite fancy her, if it wasn't for the obvious complications. "Mid-life crisis, I expect."

Sonia laughed. "So it really is goodbye, then."

"Looks like it," Tony agreed.

He had to have a leaving do, of course. Avoiding it would have involved too much fuss. A photocopied note in the internal mail advertised his availability for farewell drinks in the pub opposite the town hall on his last Friday. Everyone attended—because he wasn't disliked—but none took their coats off, because none could really call him a friend. Souvenir photos were taken (and taken great pains with, by the office's resident camera bore), and a presentation cheque (topped up by Sonia, to prevent it appearing insultingly small) was duly presented.

Tony gave the same story about the Nottingham book shop to a few pub acquaintances, and, by letter, to his landlord. He was a little put out when the landlord rang to ask for a forwarding address, but couldn't very well refuse without seeming suspicious.

"Better make it care of the shop for now, Mr. Chipping," he said, reaching for a guide to the second-hand book shops of England with his spare hand. "Hang on, I've got it here somewhere."

★ ★ ★ ★ ★

While working out his notice, he'd got to know Ian Unwin. This was essential, perhaps a little risky, but certainly not difficult. They turned out to have quite a bit in common. Ian, like Tony, was a loner. More so, if anything, really rather withdrawn, and Tony soon spotted one of the reasons why: Ian was an unadmitted homosexual.

Great, thought Tony. *He'll be glad of some sympathetic company. Discussing books, playing chess.* But he was careful to make it clear to Ian that he was a confirmed, if unprejudiced, heterosexual, so as not to arouse in the other any fears of being confronted with a decision about himself.

Their friendship proceeded very nicely, initially in lunch-hour pub sessions, and later at the bungalow in Ruislip; and after a month or so, when Tony felt he knew as much about Ian as he was ever likely to learn, or to need, he killed him.

That too was delightfully simple.

"Look, mate, sorry about this, but I really think I'm too pissed to make that last bus. You do realise that's our second bottle of scotch we're half way through?"

"No probs," said Ian—with some difficulty; though he didn't know it, he'd drunk at least four times as much as Tony. "Spare room, sofa, bath, whatever you like."

"Good man," said Tony. "In which case . . ." and he filled his host's glass to the top, one more time.

That was all it took. Getting Ian's unconscious frame through the hall and into the bath was hard work, but Tony was both fit and determined. Dragging the drowned body back out of the bath and out through the kitchen door was more exhausting than he'd anticipated, but in the end it was done.

As he dug the grave in the secluded, maturely-hedged garden (first place the police would look, of course, but in this instance they wouldn't *be* looking—no disappearance, no inquiry), Tony comforted himself with the thought that, from what he knew of his late friend, Ian would probably rather be dead, given the choice. He'd had no life to speak of, and seemed to harbour no hopes of ever finding one. Couldn't even admit what he was looking for, poor sod.

So all I've really done, Tony thought, patting the earth back into place and covering the spot with a garden bench, *is put to sleep a sad old dog who had no use for his life, and in the process secure for myself—a deserving and appreciative person—everything my own modest heart has ever longed for. A comfortable house full of books, and nothing to do all day but read them.*

The first potential crisis came quite soon: some kind of chesty, throaty thing that just wouldn't let go.

Well, why not? If anyone was entitled to be somewhat under the weather, it was him. He'd been through a lot. He'd been under a considerable strain.

Living as someone else was a little strange, Tony found, even though he had prepared himself for it so well. Bound to be, really. Not his fault, just one of those things. Even so, he eventually surrendered to the inevitable, and nervously, reluctantly, made an appointment with his—with Ian's— GP.

In the event, he could hardly contain his triumphant laughter as he left the doctor's surgery, clutching a prescription. *Bits!* The whole world was in bits! Even if there had been any risk of the doctor spotting him as an impostor, the question hadn't arisen—because the doctor had *never once taken her eyes off her computer screen!* Not even when she'd asked him if he smoked, and he'd said, "Yes, if you must know."

All the same, he took the prescription to a pharmacist a couple of bus stops away, just to be on the safe side, but really: how could a scheme like his fail, in a world like this?

Other minor alarms, potentially tricky encounters with petty officialdom, came and went, but Tony didn't panic. He always kept an emergency plan in reserve, but never needed it; and, as time went on, he began to realise that he had actually done it. He had never wanted much from life, and now he'd got it all.

Got it, and held it.

Tony was aware of a slight change in his personality. Cautiously, always cautiously, but undeniably, he was . . . well, yes, he was coming out of his shell.

The suburbs, it transpired, were not as cold and unwelcoming as he had been led to believe. Or at least, not in this cul-de-sac they weren't. Not, anyway, since his—Ian's— next-door neighbour had been replaced by June Welsh.

Never having played the romantic role, it had taken Tony a while to realise that June's almost daily poppings-round— to ask about refuse collections, to get the name of a reliable newsagent, to borrow a screwdriver—were more frequent than might be considered normal.

After they had slept together for the first time—at her place; he hadn't completely abandoned his defences— thoughts of Michelle, the clinging nuisance from his former life, drifted into his mind. But this was different. Well, *he* was different: a different name, a different life. Perhaps it was natural that he should want different things now. Want more, even.

And June was definitely different. Not as obviously attractive as Michelle, older for one thing, about Tony's age; but more of a woman, in other ways. A woman of some refinement. Not posh, not stuck-up, but thoughtful.

Quiet, like him. She was a divorcée—of a few years

standing, he gathered. Her husband had obviously hurt her (she didn't say how, and he didn't ask), and she had an air about her of emotional convalescence. And she was clearly keen on Tony.

He began to wonder if, after all, there was any real reason why he should continue to confine himself to one-night stands. Maybe, at his time of life, safe in his new existence, a steady lover might be just the thing.

He could even justify it on security grounds, without too much casuistry. A regular sexual outlet would certainly reduce the temptation to put his secret at risk through unwise pick-ups in local pubs where, for all he knew, someone might dimly recall that his face didn't fit his name. His sexual life-style had previously been a matter of choice, of personal taste, but now—in the post-Ianian period—other considerations had to take precedence.

And so June and Tony's second quiet, companionable coupling, a week after the less significant first, took place in Ian Unwin's handsome double bed (the bed in which Ian himself had been conceived, he had told Tony), and after that things took their course.

Life settled down. Marriage was never spoken of. *No need,* thought Tony, *when the holy estate of next-door-neighbourness was already so ideal.*

There were nasty moments, inevitably. He did not think of himself as a naturally dishonest man, and living a lie, in the most literal sense of the cliché, did not come easily to him. When June told him, her grey-blond head on his chest, "Ian, you just can't imagine how happy I am we found each other," he longed to say: "It's Tony. Call me Tony."

The answering machine incident was unfortunate. He had left Ian's message on the tape, and kept the machine on at all times, as one more barrier against danger. The phone rarely rang. Tony did nothing to encourage calls, and clearly Ian—despite his, in retrospect, rather pathetic investment—was not the sort who had come home daily to a spool full of urgency.

When the phone did ring that time, just as he was letting June in through the front door, it made his heart jump.

She listened to the outgoing message (there was no incoming message; a wrong number, or a frustrated salesman, presumably) with her head cocked, and then said, "Your voice sounds really weird on that. It's not like you at all."

He shrugged. "I bet even Frank Sinatra would sound like a prat on one of those things." They laughed, and the moment soon passed, but from then on Tony kept the machine's monitor volume set at zero.

Three-quarters of a year of growing happiness. Not just contentment; he was sure he knew the difference now—this was happiness.

He had his leisure, his security, his house to grow old in, his books, Ian's lump sum and pension. He had his whisky (here on the table beside him right now), he had everything he'd always dreamed of—and as if all the above wasn't more than enough, he had love as well.

Then, one night, Tony Shaw saw something on the television that revealed to him the shocking discovery that life wasn't only unfair, it was outrageously unreasonable. That no matter how modest a man's wishes, he could still never be allowed to enjoy them in peace.

There had been a row, a minor tiff. So minor, indeed, that it had ended not in shouting, but with a peck on the cheek, and the suggestion that "It might be better if we eat separately tonight, Ian, love. I'll see you in the morning."

Tony sat now, vaguely looking at the TV, planning the

exact wording of the telephonic apology he would shortly make, when a face on the screen suddenly commanded his full attention.

It was unmistakably his face, in one of the photographs, the clear, professional-quality photographs, taken at his town hall leaving do.

It was quickly replaced by a moving picture of Michelle. Clinging, thick-skinned, telegenic Michelle. Tony zapped up the sound.

". . . leaving his fiancée, Michelle Knight, fearing the worst. Michelle: the most awful thing must be just not knowing?"

He killed the sound again. He didn't need to hear what had happened, it was already unfolding in his mind:

1. Michelle, convinced that he would never leave her without a word, had called at his flat. Somehow made contact with the landlord, been told that letters forwarded to Nottingham had been returned Not Known At This Address.

2. Had gone to his former workplace, where his puzzled boss, Sonia, had helpfully unearthed a copy of the farewell photo.

3. Had received little help from the police, who were not interested in disappearances of healthy, adult men when there were no suggestions of suspicious circumstances.

4. Had approached the production company responsible for *Lost and Found,* where her good looks, her obvious sincerity, and her romantic fantasies had struck a chord with a researcher bored with stories of missing dads and runaway teenagers.

5. And the rest was history.

And even as this list (file under *End of the World*) unfurled behind his eyes, the greater part of Tony's mind was filled with just two thoughts:

1. Is June sitting next door, watching this programme?
2. And if she is, what the hell am I going to do about it?

★ ★ ★ ★ ★

One of the interesting results of putting together a collection of stories which were written over several years is discovering recurring themes, which I wasn't conscious of at the time (a less pleasing aspect of the process is that it draws my attention to various repetitions, verbal tics, and—to put it bluntly—obsessions). This story (which first appeared in Martin Edwards's 1996 CWA annual, *Perfectly Criminal*) is another one about specious moral logic, in which a man manages to convince himself that it's all right to do something self-evidently wrong, due to extenuating circumstances.

Many people, of course, long to give up their day jobs, so that they can spend all their time reading (or perhaps writing), instead of wasting most of their waking hours on wage-slavery. It may even be that you are one of them. If so, I can only hope that your sense of right and wrong is a little more solidly grounded than Tony's!

OLD SULTAN

No one had ever called Sultan a nice guy. He didn't even think of himself—on those very rare occasions when he thought about himself at all—as a nice guy.

But loyal, yes. He thought of himself as loyal, and he thought that others thought of him that way, too. You didn't have to be nice to do his job, was the way Sultan looked at it, but you did have to be loyal.

And here was the thing: it had never occurred to him that loyalty didn't go both ways. Just never occurred to him.

"So how do you know he's going to kill you?" said Wolf, and Sultan thought—*What sort of dumb question is that? Wolf's in the business, he knows how these things work.*

"What else is he going to do, Wolfie? Give me a pension? Throw me a retirement party? Buy me a cottage by the seaside?"

"OK, he's going to kill you." Wolf shrugged his gym-built shoulders, his long, curly, sun-blond hair rattling around his sunbed-orange face.

"He's going to kill me," said Sultan. "That's what I been telling you, he is going to kill me, and that is just totally unfair. That is just totally out of order. Twenty-three years, one mistake, and—*blam.*"

"The old lead handshake," said Wolf.

"He's going to kill me," said Sultan. "Is that a bastard or what?"

"He's a bastard," Wolf nodded. "Geoff Shepherd is an ungrateful bastard."

"No, no." Sultan shook his bullet-shaped, crew-cut head, spilt a little beer on his barrel chest, wiped it off with his ham hands, so that it flicked downwards, onto his big gut, which looked like it might have been fat or might have been muscle. "No, that's where you're wrong—Mr. Shepherd isn't a bastard. The situation is a bastard, but Mr. Shepherd . . . he's a good boss, Wolfie, he really is. It's been a privilege to serve him these twenty-three years, and the only thing I want in the world is to serve him for another twenty-three."

"Well, yeah, I take your point," said Wolf. "But I mean, come on, man—one mistake, you'd think he could live with that, wouldn't you? Bloke that rich, what does it matter?"

The pub, in Covent Garden, was empty. Full of people, so packed it'd take a bomb scare to clear a space at the bar, but as far as Sultan and Wolf were concerned it was empty: full of nothing people, tourists, office workers. Zombies. No one they knew ever drank here, no one from Sultan's arena in north London, or Wolf's south of the river. They could talk as loud as they liked; no one who mattered a damn would hear a damn.

"Three hundred thousand pounds, Wolfie, that's what I cost Mr. Shepherd last Saturday."

"It happens," shrugged Wolf. He was in the same line of work: sheep-dogging people, merchandise. Ten years younger than Sultan, nowhere near as experienced, but still, basically off the same shelf. He knew you couldn't get it right every time.

"Never happened to me," said Sultan. "Never happened to Mr. Shepherd, neither, not since I been with him. And I been with him pretty much since the start."

And another difference between the two of them: Wolf

didn't take the stubborn pride in his work that Sultan did, didn't go for all this old-shit loyalty stuff. It was a living, that's all. If you're big, you don't lose your bottle, and you can keep your mouth shut—yeah, a *good* living. But just a living, not some sort of bleedin' *religion*.

"You got a number of choices," said Wolf, getting down to business, growing mildly irritated by his friend's company. Hell—*friend*. Professional acquaintance would be more like it. If poor old Sultan wanted to do something about all this, fine, Wolf could see a way. But if he was just looking for someone to whine to, let him buy a woman with big ears.

"Choice number one," he said, hoping the big fool was listening, because he wasn't going to say this twenty times. "You get him before he gets you."

"No," said Sultan, and that was the end of that.

"OK, choice number two. You do a runner."

"Where to?" said Sultan, and Wolf realised, with another flicker of annoyance, that the question wasn't rhetorical.

"Hell, *wherever*, man! You got family somewhere, yeah? Friends, whatever. Or, better yet, somewhere where nobody knows you, start again. Spain, America, Eastern Europe."

"I don't want to go," said Sultan, and that, too, was that.

"Right," said Wolf, leaning in, getting serious now. "You want to keep your job, yeah? OK then, there's only one way we can fix that."

"He says it's because I'm too old," said Sultan.

"I know, man, you told me. Too old to do the business anymore. That's crap, man, and you're going to prove it."

"I heard him talking about it with that poofter son of his. Too old, getting past it, got to go."

"Yes," said Wolf. "Now listen to me: the poofter son, Tony—am I right in thinking you don't have the same feelings of loyalty to Tony as you do to his father, yeah?"

"I don't give a toss about Tony," said Sultan. So, hell, he *had* been listening. Well, well, you just never could tell.

"Good," said Wolf. "In that case, go get us a couple of pints and I'll make a couple of phone calls, and pretty soon all your troubles will be behind you."

For a further hour, they discussed details. At no point in the conversation did Sultan say "Thanks" to Wolf, for all the trouble he was going to on Sultan's behalf.

Loyalty: you were loyal to your boss, your friends, family if you'd got one, and that was that. Thanks didn't come into it.

"OK, Tony—get in the car."

"Who the hell are you?" said Tony, in that second-generation-money accent to which Wolf, himself, aspired in vain.

"You don't ask, you don't find out," said Wolf. "And if you don't find out, you don't get killed. All right?" It was pretty dark here, and pretty deserted, but even so—a thing like this, you don't want to hang about, take your time over it. If the guy has time to think, to work it out, to say to himself, *He's not going to kill me,* and just walk away . . .

"This *is* a gun in my hand, by the way," Wolf added. "Just in case you thought it was something else, and the crime under way here was, maybe, indecent exposure. It isn't, Tony, it's kidnapping. Now get in the bloody car!"

Tony got in. What the hell, his dad would sort it out.

"You know who's got him?" Geoff Shepherd's voice was frankly incredulous.

"Not exactly *know,* Mr. Shepherd," said Sultan. "But I am sure I can find out. I am sure I can get him back for you. There's no-one knows north London like I know it, Mr. Shepherd, you know yourself that's true."

Provided they're keeping my son in a pub, thought Shepherd. But then, none of his other people seemed to have a clue about this. It had come from nowhere—who the hell would snatch Geoff Shepherd's son? Who could possibly be that crazy? "All right, Sultan, listen." He'd had plans for Sultan— plans for that very day, in fact—but they could wait. The old dog wasn't going anywhere, too stupid to run. He'd let him do this, sniff around, come up with nothing, and then he'd take care of him.

No hurry.

"Yes, Mr. Shepherd?" said Sultan, eagerly.

"You do what you can. And if you find him . . . well, obviously, if you do find him, Sultan, I'll be very grateful. Most grateful indeed." Which was true. A son is a son after all, no matter how big a waste of space he might be.

Three nights later, Sultan watched from across the road as Wolf deposited a heavily doped Tony Shepherd in the disused beer cellar of a gay club in Soho. After a while, Wolf came out of the cellar and gave Sultan the thumbs up.

Sultan waited five, ten minutes. Made love to the shadows, smoked a cigarette. Kept watch.

Nothing moved: nobody on the plot.

He ground out his cigarette, and set to work with the bolt-cutters. Easy job, didn't even sweat, but it'd look like he'd had a struggle, should anyone ever come checking. Which he doubted: the club was an independent, its security guy just happened to be unlucky enough to owe Wolf a favour. There was nothing here to lead Mr. Shepherd to his son's kidnappers.

"Tony! Tony, you there, son?" Sultan shouted into the mildewed darkness. "Tony, it's OK mate, it's me—Sultan."

A groan. Sultan took out his penlight, called again, received another answering groan, navigated towards a far corner.

There—lying on the stone floor, his ankles cuffed to his wrists: "London's most ineligible bachelor," as Mr. Shepherd sometimes referred to his son. The heir to one of the capital's most successful, and fastest-growing, and most rapidly-modernising business empires.

"Tony? You alive, mate? It's me, Sultan. You're all right now, I've come to take you home."

Still blindfolded, still groggy, the heir cocked his head towards his saviour's voice. "Who the hell are you?" he croaked.

"Sultan," said Sultan.

"Who the holy shit is Sultan?" said Tony, sounding deeply unimpressed.

Who am I? thought Sultan. *Who am I? Not only am I the man who's just saved your life, you little prat, I have also been one of your father's most loyal employees since before you were born!* He felt blood burning in his ears. *You want to learn to take a bit more interest in your inheritance, boy!*

And then—because, after all, his loyalty was to the father, not the son—Sultan drew back his booted foot and let it fly, nice and hard, into Tony's stomach.

"Oi, you!" cried Sultan. "Get out of it!" He stumbled about the cellar, banging into walls, grunting and groaning, wrestling with an invisible opponent. The fight ended in the slamming of the door, and Sultan leaned down to place a solicitous hand on Tony's shoulder. "Christ, you all right, son? One of the bastards must've been still hanging around—he got that kick in before I could stop him. You all right?"

"Now I know who Sultan is," Tony said, as if to himself. "He's the fat stupid one."

Sultan's foot was half way back through its swing, when he

stopped it —with an effort, and with the thought that, *No, one kick was for free, but two and the little sod'd be sure to rumble him, dope or no dope.*

Instead, he picked the boy up, threw him over his shoulders, and carried him out to the back seat of the car. A mile or so later, he pulled in to an empty pub car park and removed Tony's blindfold.

The heir opened his eyes, one by one, blinked, gobbed up a blatant lump of blood-smeared phlegm, and raised his eyes to see the face of the man who'd come to deliver him to his father's wrath.

"Took your time, didn't you?" he sneered. "And I don't suppose you thought to bring a flask with you, huh? *Sultan?*"

Sultan stared at him. Hating him. *The things I do for my boss,* he thought.

"Tell you what, lad," he said. "You behave yourself and I won't tell your dad where I found you."

That had the little bastard white-faced all the way home.

Sultan enjoyed the moment. Another thing his job, his life, had taught him: enjoy the moment. You get up in the morning and you've still got your face, you're ahead of the game.

For three weeks, Sultan enjoyed the moment.

And then Wolf turned up, one night, smiling and licking his lips.

Sultan, back in his master's good books—in better books, if the truth be told, than he'd been in for some years—was baby-sitting one of Mr. Shepherd's young executives taking delivery of a consignment of merchandise at a road cafe near Heathrow airport.

The deal made, the young executive slapped Sultan on the back, said "Won't be a mo, Granddad, just nipping to the gents," and left Sultan, and the merchandise, sitting in the firm's BMW in the cafe car park.

Which was when Wolf rapped on the passenger-side window.

Sultan didn't jump out of his skin. You did that in his line of work, and you were dead. But as he leaned over to crack the window open, keeping his right hand carefully out of view, he did have to concentrate on his breathing just a bit. Especially when he saw who was there.

"Hell did you spring from?" he said, trying to imagine the kind of innocent coincidence that might have brought Wolf to this same car park on this same night.

Wolf, long tongue running over dry lips, got straight down to business. "There's ten separately wrapped units in that package, Sultan," he said. "I only need one of them."

Ah, right, thought Sultan. He nodded to himself: there's no such thing as coincidence, Mr. Shepherd often said, and as usual, Mr. Shepherd had been proved right.

"Come on, Sultan," Wolf wheedled, his over-shoulder glances increasingly edgy. "You owe me, don't you? You don't deny that?"

"All right," said Sultan, unlocking the passenger's door, sliding over to get out on that side. This time he didn't bother hiding the gun, as he slipped it into his waistband.

"Good man!" Wolf crowed, and then gasped, as his fat, stupid, sometime pal stepped out of the car, and, seemingly in the same motion, picked him up by his hair and his balls.

"In case you was wondering," Sultan said, carrying Wolf over to a bank of metal mesh litter bins at the far side of the car park, "it's muscle, not fat. Just in case you was wondering."

While Wolf lay, winded in body and spirit, amid the burger boxes and the hardened blobs of chewing gum, they both heard a car squeal off into the night.

"Looks like you lost your lift," said Sultan. "You got money for a cab?"

Wolf nodded.

"OK then," said Sultan, walking briskly back to the BMW. He turned once, to say, in a quiet but carrying voice: "I do owe you, Wolfie, that's right. And one day I will repay you. But I'll tell you when, all right?"

The junior executive got back in the car moments after Sultan. "All cool on the Western Front?" he chirped.

"Yeah," said Sultan, foot on the pedal.

It shocked Sultan that Wolf didn't give up after that. Really shocked him. "Know when to go for it, know when to call it a day"—how often had he heard Mr. Shepherd say that? That was the trouble with blokes like Wolfie—no mentors, no education. Different generation.

Wolf's second approach was, by his standards, a little more subtle.

In a pub full of Greek Cypriots in Crouch End, Sultan sat one Saturday lunchtime, more than a month after his daring rescue of Tony Shepherd from the still unidentified hands of his kidnappers. He was watching the dart players, enjoying a quiet pint and that particular restfulness which he sometimes found in the company of people he didn't know, when the bench he was sitting on sagged under the weight of a bodybuilder's arse.

"Listen," said Wolf, without preliminaries. "Sorry about that crap the other night."

"Forget it," said Sultan, and the way he said it—firm rather than dismissive—made it clear that he was not employing a mere cliché.

"No, look," said Wolf, leaning his mousse-scented lion's

mane into Sultan's neck, putting his mouth next to Sultan's ear. "I went about it all wrong. You had every right to slap me. I was being crude, I wasn't thinking. All right? Apology accepted?"

Sultan said nothing beyond a murmured "Good arrows, son," addressed to a player who'd just stuck in a three-dart finish while his opponent was still warming up.

"Thing is, Sultan, I know what you were thinking, and you're totally correct—doing it that way, you're just going to get yourself into trouble. And I don't want that. Do I? After all the trouble I went to before, getting you out of trouble. Hey?"

No response.

"Point is, though," Wolf continued, because he'd come here to say his piece, and no dumb act was going to stop him. "Point is, man, a favour deserves a favour. Yeah? So this time I got a plan, a proper plan, and I just need you to help me out."

Sultan hadn't looked at Wolf since he sat down. He didn't now, as he said, quietly, "I'll help you out that fucking window, you don't do as I say and forget it."

Wolf stood up. "All I need," he said, "is for you to go blind and deaf for about thirty seconds. That's all. And then we're quits. I'll be in touch."

And he was. Two more chance meetings, a phone call—even, for God's sake, a letter, sent to Sultan's home address! Sultan couldn't remember the last time he'd had a letter. Nobody wrote to Sultan, not even the government. Not even American Express.

This had to stop.

"Thanks for agreeing to a meet, man. I mean it," said Wolf, buckling his belt in the passenger seat of the BMW. "I truly appreciate this. And listen, before you say anything, I just want to say this, right? This can work for us. You and me, we're two of a kind, Sultan, and this thing can work *big* for us. And the beauty of it is, no one need ever know. Because I've worked it out, yeah? What I figure is—"

Sultan hadn't buckled his seat belt. He leant down, produced the gun from under the driver's seat.

"This is what *I've* worked out, Wolfie," he said.

"Oh God," whispered Wolf. "You're not . . ."

He said nothing more, just stared at the gun, and Sultan felt sure there wasn't going to be any fighting here. Just in case, though, he looked right into Wolf's eyes and said, "Muscle, remember? Not fat."

Wolf hardly resisted at all as Sultan locked him in the boot of the car.

Sultan got back in, lit a cigarette, fastened his seat belt. Pulled out into the weekend traffic, and made for the motorway.

He only stopped once on the long drive, at a service station three hours into the journey.

He got out, walked round the car, banged on the lid of the boot. "You alive?" he said.

"Listen, Sultan—"

"Right," said Sultan. He got back in, buckled up, drove on.

Looking at Wolf now, naked, sitting on his bare bum on the damp soil, Sultan could see he was nothing special.

Younger? Yeah sure, he was younger and prettier than Sultan. But then, so was a newborn baby. You can get a body from a gym, Sultan thought, but you can't get an education. You can't learn the rules. Only experience teaches those kind of lessons.

At least the man was smart enough not to run. Unless he wasn't being smart, just tough. Either way, here in what must be pretty damn close to the exact geographical middle of nowhere, Wolf had stripped at Sultan's command, had sat at Sultan's command, had remained still at Sultan's command.

Still except for the shivering, and Sultan could hardly blame him for that. Dusk had fallen long since, and they didn't go in for warm nights in deepest, unspoilt Scotland.

"I thought you helped me because that was what friends did," Sultan told Wolf, speaking slowly, speaking loudly, trying to make this foolish, vain apprentice understand the way things worked. "I thought you was being loyal to me, because we were mates. I didn't know that you was doing it so that I would have to do something for you."

Wolf said nothing. He knew there was nothing worth saying now, in this place and time. He just wished it was over. He just wished he had something to drink: cold always made him thirsty. Cold and fear both.

"But OK," Sultan continued, scratching his spiky chin with the hand that wasn't holding the gun. "You thought you were doing me a favour, you thought I owed you one, you don't know what loyalty means. All right then, we'll play by your rules. I *do* owe you one, and now I'm going to pay it back."

Wolf managed a wispy laugh. "Some favour, fat man."

Sultan didn't reply. Just stuck the gun in his jacket pocket, began walking back to the car, parked uninhabited miles away.

"What—where are you—what are you doing, man?" For the first time in hours, Wolf didn't feel that he was minutes away from death; and—it was weird, but—he kind of felt like he'd been stood up on a date.

Sultan turned, walked slowly backwards as he said: "You

stay there until I'm out of sight. Then it's up to you. You and I have no further business."

Wolf stumbled to his feet, fell to earth again as his cramped legs collapsed. "I'll die out here, man! No clothes, no water—I'll bloody die out here, you fat bastard!" And then, more reasonably, he added: "At least give me my contact lenses back!"

"If I ever see you again," said Sultan, "in London or anywhere else, I will kill you dead. No discussion, just *blam*. Got that?"

Sultan *was* almost out of sight, before it struck him that he was leaving unfinished business behind him. Had he really taught Wolfie the lesson he so badly wanted him to learn? Unsure, he retraced his steps.

There was Wolfie, still sitting there. He looked a mess. Stinking, from his long imprisonment in the car. Wretched, from his predicament. His face filthy with tear tracks. His hair still looked good, though, you had to give him that.

He looked up at Sultan's approach, and started crying again. "I knew you'd be back, you fat bastard."

"I wanted to make sure you understood. If I ever see you again I *will* kill you. Not to punish you, or to shut you up, or because I'm scared of you, or any of that crap. But because it would mean that you'd been disloyal to me. It would mean that you'd done me a favour, I'd done you one by return, and then you'd turned round and flung it back in my face."

Satisfied now, he turned and walked away again. This time he didn't look back.

He was busy thinking: Loyalty—it works both ways, and in all directions. If you don't know that, then what's the point of getting out of bed in the morning?

Now to go home and work out a way of teaching the same lesson to Mr. Shepherd.

★ ★ ★ ★ ★

I was invited to write a story based on one of Grimm's fairy tales, for an anthology, and this is what I came up with— eventually. It was hard work. I'd never read Grimm before, and was somewhat surprised to discover just how dull the tales were, plotless and inconsequential. Honestly, I think the stories in *Once Upon a Crime* (1998, edited by Ed Gorman and Martin Greenberg) were a great improvement on the originals!

I misinterpreted the brief slightly; I didn't realise we were allowed to give our stories new titles, so I stuck to "Old Sultan." I'm not sure what I might have called it, otherwise; "Do Who You Would Be Done By," possibly.

TWELVE OF THE LITTLE BUGGERS

Middle of September, one of my editors rang—would I like to do a jokey piece on cats?

"Cats?" I said.

"Right," said Jenni. "Like, we were talking it over in the office, and we thought, you know—robins, turkeys, reindeer, etc., etc, puddings . . ."

I couldn't immediately see the connection. "Puddings?" I said.

"Right," said Jenni. "I mean, only three more planning months to Christmas, right?"

"Oh," I said, "the Christmas number. Gotcha."

"Right," said Jenni. "So we thought—no: let's do cats. Not very Christmassy, but, you know, different. Cute. Nice big puddy-tat on the cover. Lots of interior pics, lots of colour. Kittens peeking playfully out of Christmas stockings. Lovely tabby mummy-cats posing proudly on Yuletide logs. Sweet old toms dozing amid the prezzies, 'neath the glittering tree. And then, seasonal cat stories. Tragic tales of cats given as gifts, but with, like, happy endings. A hundred and one things you can buy your kitty for Christmas. Recipes—"

"Instead of turkey?"

She laughed one of those editorial laughs; the very short sort, because even if editors had a sense of humour, they certainly wouldn't have time to indulge it with only three planning months left before Christmas.

192

I've only met Jenni once in the flesh—what there is of it. She really doesn't have anything much but teeth; that and a slight lisp, which is, in fact, so slight that I tend to doubt its authenticity. First time she commissioned me, she took me to lunch at a reasonably fashionable West End Italian place. I drank imported beer; she ordered mineral water. She asked the waiter for a yoghurt—a *main course* yoghurt, right?—and seemed pretty surprised when he told her they didn't have any yoghurt. So she just ate bread sticks instead.

I ordered the whole menu.

I could tell now, by listening to her on the phone, that she had that habit of twisting her professionally-frazzled hair around her fingers while she spoke; not from coquetry, though, but from repressed, generalised irritation.

"Special celebration recipes. What to feed Tiddles while the family's enjoying the mince pies."

"Yes, I get it," I said, in case she thought I was still confused.

"And, of course, humour."

"Of course," I said. That's what I do: I write humour for humourless magazines. Been doing it all my life. I could have done something else, I suppose. Could have become a mercenary, for instance, but I didn't fancy the training.

"So we thought, you know, Jim Potter. Jim's our man for a spot of cat humour."

"I'm flattered." I wasn't.

"Well," said Jenni, "you're the best, Jim." I wasn't. "We were thinking, you know, urban cats. An A-Z feature, maybe. Or a 'Twenty Crazy Things You Never Knew About.' Or whatever you like."

"Fine," I said. "How many words you want?"

"Well, we were thinking, you know, you could go to twelve, maybe. Or eight, with a big photo."

"I'll do eight," I said. Jenni's magazine pays a flat rate, not according to word-count. "When do you need the copy?"

"Ummm . . . how about yesterday?" she asked, playfully.

"Tricky," I replied, coyly.

"OK. Week tomorrow?"

"No prob."

"By the way, Jim, I ought to check—you have got a cat yourself? Only if you haven't, you know, sorry, I should have said . . ."

"Oh yeah," I said.

"Oh really? That's great! I thought you must have. We've got this survey in the Christmas issue, says that men in their thirties living alone are almost always cat persons."

"Oh yeah," I said. "Matter of fact, I've got twelve of the little buggers."

"Twelve!" she squealed. "That's great! You must really love cats!"

The girl's a genius.

I wrote the piece the next day—"Urban Cats: An Unreliable History"—then waited a week until the deadline was up, and faxed it through. Jenni rang to say she loved it. Then she rang again ten minutes later, and said my "stuff" was so fabulous, she was putting it on the cover. More money, obviously. Quite a lot more, you know, money. Actually.

"And then we were talking about it, and we thought—you know, let's get some pics."

"Great," I said.

"You know," she said, "of your cats. All twelve of them. Wouldn't that be great?"

"Oh yeah," I said.

"Great! So, listen, no time to waste, I'll send a photographer round this afternoon, OK? About five, five-thirty?"

"Oh yeah," I said. "Great."

Then we rang off, and I thought: Jesus-in-a-manger—where am I supposed to get twelve cats from, by five o'clock this afternoon?

The woman at the cat rescue centre wasn't all that helpful. "You want to provide a new home for *twelve* cats?"

"No, hell, that's the last thing I want to do, I don't even like cats. I just want to borrow them for a couple of hours. Really, they'll be back there before anyone notices they've gone."

"You want to *borrow* twelve cats?"

"Listen, don't get hung up on the number. Half a dozen'd probably do. I could say they'd eaten the others."

"You want to borrow *six* cats?"

"Yeah. One thing; do you deliver? I'm a bit tied up this afternoon, that would really be a great help."

"I don't know if this is some kind of joke, or what, but I think you don't understand what we do here. This isn't Feline Express. We don't keep a fleet of moonlighting students on mopeds, biking Cats-With-Everything direct to your door, thirty minutes max or your money back. We don't—what I'm trying to say is—we don't *lend* cats. OK? This isn't the National Whiskers Library."

I thought that over for a moment. "Look, if it's a matter of money, I'd be more than happy to put a couple of quid in the collecting tin. Or in your own, private collecting tin, if that'd be better."

And then, while she was telling me that she hoped we might meet one day, because she knew a vet who could be relied upon to keep his scissors open and his mouth shut, I suddenly remembered the allotments.

I don't do gardening myself (as you'll know if you've ever

read my column, "How Not To Do Gardening," in *Gardener's Week Magazine*), but the quickest route from my house to the pub is via a footpath that runs alongside a little river, right past the allotments—and even I know what an allotment site is: a patch of wasteland, divided up into strips which the local council rents out to residents, mostly old people and food faddists, so that they can grow their own fruit and veggies there. Though why anyone should want to bother, when they're lucky enough to live in a country with perfectly good burger-bars conveniently situated on every street corner, is far beyond my powers of explanation.

The point is, however, this: what did I often see on those allotments, on my way to and from the boozerama? Cats. I saw cats. Loads of them. Stray cats, presumably. Well, either that, or gardening cats.

Never having had a cat, I didn't know what kind of gear you needed to catch them. So I just grabbed everything I could think of: a big sack, a length of wood, a tin of date-expired treacle, a box of candles, and a whistle.

Took me two hours. Partly, that was because I kept losing count. It's not easy—and if you ever have anything to do with cats yourself, you might want to remember this—it's not easy to count cats in a big sack. Eventually, I had a brainwave: what did it matter if I got too many cats? I mean, if there were thirteen of them, I could just tell the photographer that one of the little buggers had had a baby, right?

Don't ask me to describe the cats. They were various colours. I don't know what you call cat colours. Some were sort of splodgy, some sort of spotty, some sort of stripy. And some were sort of, sort of splodgy, sort of spotty, and sort of stripy all at once. They were various sizes.

They were cats anyway, so I took them home.

I just about reached the gate, when all of a sudden there was a man standing in front of me, holding his arms out like a recently-demoted traffic cop. I didn't like the look of him: a long, cruel face, a superior scowl. Fair enough, though—he obviously didn't like the look of me, either.

"What have you got in that sack?"

"In the sack?"

"What's moving about in your sack?"

"Oh, yeah. Tortoises," I explained.

"*Tortoises?*" Like he didn't believe me.

"Certainly," I said. "Just picked 'em up in those woods back there."

Trying to edge round me, trying to get a good squeeze at my cat-sack, he said: "There are no tortoises in those woods, for heaven's sake."

"Of course there aren't," I said, "I got them all in this sack."

"What for?" he sneered.

"For? Why, for my three kids, naturally. They love tortoises, but the way they get through them, I can't afford to keep buying them. Kids, huh? So I thought: Hey, Do It Yourself!"

He sneered on, in silence.

"So I'm taking them home for . . . for little Gerald," I said. "And . . ." The man waited. "And for little Geraldine."

"That's only *two* children," he said, unpleasantly.

"Well, not really," I said, "because you see, the third one's also called Geraldine, due to, like, y'know, a mix-up at the hospital."

He started to say something that apparently began with "*You—*" but then he stopped, and I realised he was staring over my shoulder. Turning round, I saw in the distance, back by the entrance to the woods, a young, scruffy guy in a combat jacket, striding towards us.

"You just stay away from those cats. Got it?" And with that, the interrogation was broken off, as the long-faced vigilante disappeared through a gap in the bushes.

Weird behavior. But then, once people let cats into their lives, they do strange things. That is a medical fact.

Home safe, with about thirty minutes to spare, I unleashed the cats. Then I poured a gigantic vodka, lit a small cigar, and relaxed.

Carl, the pointlessly enthusiastic, ponytailed lensman—bright orange shirt, collar size XXL—was pretty impressed with my cats. "Great cats!" he said. "They're so—I dunno, they're so wild, aren't they?"

"Oh yeah," I said. "They really are."

"They just never keep still for a moment, do they? Rushing around like crazy things!"

"Oh yeah," I said. "Thing is, they're not really used to company."

"No?"

"Not really. I tend to ignore them, myself."

"OK! Look, do you think you could get them, sort of, all together in one place? You know, so I can do the old clickety-click?"

"Well," I said. "It's like you said yourself: they're pretty wild cats."

"Maybe if you fed them?"

"Brilliant!" I said. "That's a brilliant idea. Um . . . you got any mice, or anything?"

The photographer laughed—rather meaninglessly, I thought. "Might be easier if you just, you know, opened a can or something."

"Oh yeah," I said. "Good thinking." So I opened a few

cans, emptied the contents into a plastic washing-up bowl, and put the bowl on the kitchen floor. Sure enough, the cats came running.

"That is amazing," said Carl.

"Must've been hungry," I said.

"Yeah, but—chili con carne? I never knew cats ate chili con carne."

"Oh yeah," I explained. "Your cat, you see, your average cat is a big meat-eater."

He laughed again, and started setting up his lights. "Well, they obviously love it. And I can see you love your cats, too. That tinned chili costs a lot more than cat food."

Cat food, I thought. *Damn.*

An hour later, he'd gone ("Listen, if you ever decide you've got too many cats," he said on the doorstep, "my little girl . . ."—"Don't worry," I said, "you'll be the first to hear"), and it was over.

Just call me Mr. Resourceful.

It wasn't over.

Once the photographer's car had disappeared around the corner, I loaded up the old sack again, and set off once more for the allotments. I whistled as I walked, light of heart though heavily burdened.

I didn't meet anyone on my short journey, except a comedian in a milkman's tunic, who told me: "You want to change your butcher, pal. That meat's wriggling."

Back amongst the beans and squashes, I shook out the sack, and out tumbled the cats. They sat there on the ground, looking at me, but they didn't look for long. They couldn't, because I wasn't there for long.

Late that night, a crashing sound woke me. By the time I got downstairs, there were three cats sitting in my hallway, making cat noises. Even as I stood there, another two appeared through a small, flapped hole in the door (which I'd previously supposed was there for the benefit of shortsighted postmen).

I hastily gathered up a couple of cats, and opened the door. That was a mistake. The cats in my arms screeched, scratched, and then leapt back into the house. A cat which had been in the process of using the hole when I opened the door, and which was now swinging there like a magician's assistant interrupted in the middle of a sawing-the-lady-in-half trick, just screeched. And all the cats outside, who had been queuing patiently for the hole, dashed past me with the odd chirrup of appreciation at my good manners.

Right, I thought. Deep breaths. Go about this logically.

I found a bit of stiff cardboard, and taped it over the hole. I retrieved my trusty sack, and carried it up to my bedroom. There I found three cats: one under the bed, one already asleep inside the bed, and another squatting vulgarly on top of the wardrobe. Not without some difficulty, and a few minor wounds, I achieved their ensackment.

Then I left the bedroom, shutting the door firmly behind me, and emptied the captured cats out onto the street. There was no way I was visiting the allotments at this time of night, dressed only in boxer shorts and a pair of mock-leather slippers.

I repeated this operation in each room, methodically, and then, exhausted and slightly bleeding, went back to my bedroom.

Which now contained four cats.

It was a hot night, and I'd left most of the windows in the house open. Not open enough for burglars; but, evidently, open enough for cats.

I started over.

I have a vague memory of myself, at some stage in that eternal, furry night, standing in the hall with a bottle of vodka in one hand and a box of Elastoplast in the other, singing *"Close the doors, they're coming in the windows! Close the windows, they're coming in the doors!"*

I don't know if you've ever been in one of those situations where you're trying to shove a number of small jellies up a wide drainpipe? I know I haven't. I don't suppose anybody ever has, actually, but if by some extraordinarily unlikely chance you know what I'm talking about, then you'll know exactly how I felt.

Late morning, crusty on the sofa, I awoke to discover I still had the vodka, I still had the sticking plaster, and I still had a house full of cats. Twelve of the little buggers.

Obviously, clearing them out one by one, or even sack by sack, wasn't going to do it. They'd probably just hang around the front door, and I'd never be able to go outside again for fear of inviting reinfestation. No, what I needed here was a permanent solution.

So I called my Aunty Cissie.

Aunty Cissie is eighty-seven, and to my certain knowledge she's been dead three years. I should know: I was at her funeral.

"Jim, my dear! You good boy, you've just rung up to see how I am."

"Now then, Aunty. You know I only ring when I want something." Incapable of hearing harsh truth without disbelieving it, my Aunty Cissie; podgy, breathless, sagging, permanently on the homeward leg of a return trip to doolallyland. Or do I mean a jolly, rotund, chuckle-faced, happy-golucky senior citizen? No, I don't.

"Do you know, I haven't seen you for three years?" she

said, as delightedly as she said everything. "Not since your
Great Uncle Norman's funeral."

"Oh, right," I said. Now I come to think of it, it might not
have been her funeral. Might have been somebody else's. I
don't remember; I didn't stay long. "So you're still alive,
then?"

She chuckled. "Just about, dear. You are sweet. I know
how you worry about me."

"Mm-mm," I said. I don't like to commit myself too
strongly over the phone, you never know who's listening.
"Look, Aunty. You know about cats. You ever heard of cats
. . . adopting people?"

"Oh yes, they'll do that, dear. If their old owners have got
a new baby, or a new kitten, or a new computer game. Cats
demand attention, and they won't tolerate rivals. Or if
they've been mistreated, or living rough, or they're not getting the kind of food they like. I had a cat once that wouldn't
eat anything but Chinese stir-fried mushrooms."

"How about twelve at once? Mass defection—you ever
hear of a case like that?"

"Oh, dear! Is that what you've got? Twelve of the little
buggers! Well, I'm not surprised. You always were a gentle
boy. They must all be in love with you!"

Just my luck, I thought. *In a world full of seventeen-year-old
nymphos . . .*

"Still," said Aunty Cissie. "They're company, aren't they?
And we all need company, don't we, now and then?"

Oh, God . . .

"Which reminds me, dear. When are you coming to see
me? How about next week?"

"No, sorry, I'm pretty busy next week. And the week after.
But you're right, we must make a definite date. Tell you
what, I'll come round one day next year."

"Oh, that is kind of you dear. I shall count the hours! Oh, but Jim?" she added, as I began the long process of hanging up. "Don't make it a Thursday."

"Not a Thursday, Aunty. Right you are."

"No, dear. You see, Thursday's my night for going to the lavatory."

So, there you are. Cat psychology is pretty simple really, once you know what you're doing. And what I did was this: I didn't feed them, and I removed the cardboard from the hole. And after twenty-four hours of involuntary hunger-striking, they forgot the taste of chili con carne, began to wonder what they were doing here, and one by one slipped off back to the allotments—having first peed on every available surface, and in every imaginable crevice. I could have rented out the house as a rehabilitation centre for the nasally-disadvantaged.

Anyway, it was over.

Until Jenni rang again.

"Jim—the pics are totally fabulous! What we thought was, we'd like to blow one of your cats up."

"Blow them all up if you like," I said, pleased to hear so sensible a suggestion from so unexpected a source.

"For the cover," she said. "That gingery one with the kinky tail—you know which one I mean?"

Was there a gingery one? "Oh yeah," I said.

"Great! So, like, what do you call her?"

"Stinking rat," I said.

"Stinking *what?*"

"Er—no, no. Not stinking. Slinking. Slinking Cat."

"Oh, that's *sweet.*"

"Slinky for short."

"Oh, that is *so* sweet!"

"Oh yeah," I said. "Well, she's a sweet cat. Glad you like her."

"*Love* her," said Jenni. "In fact, what we were thinking was, you know, why don't we send Carl over again, get him to do some more pics? Just of Slinky, you know, make a bit of a feature of her."

"Great," I said. "Some more pics. Great idea."

"Well, you know, we're talking about maybe even a calendar. You know, like a spin-off. She's really a special little puss. My publisher's own personal idea, actually. First one he's had for ages! Whoops, no, he's, you know, smashing, actually. Anyway, if it works out, we could actually pay you some, you know, truly decent money for once. I mean, the publisher's just given me this cheque with, like, a signature at the bottom and nothing else! So, what do you think, Jim?"

"Oh yeah," I said. "Totally fabulous."

A flashlight. A writer on the edge of madness. The allotments by night.

"Slinky . . . Slinky . . . C'mere, Slinky . . ."

What the hell was I calling her *Slinky* for, for God's sake?

Yup, that was Slinky all right. Sitting on my bed, eating chili con carne from a plastic washing-up bowl. I could tell by comparing her with the big photo Jenni had faxed me. Good old Slinky, my sweet little, special little golden goose.

There was a knock on the door.

The man now standing in my hall was angry. He was also fiftyish, well-dressed, greyly bald, and the same bony bloke who'd doubted my tortoises on the allotments the other day. But mostly he was angry.

"It's *my* cat, Mr. Potter. You have stolen my cat, and I

demand its return. Without any further argument. Understand?"

"Must be some mistake, Dr. Lane. My little Slinky and me, we—"

"Look! I saw you take the damn cat. From the allotments. I was down there looking for her—because she was missing, right? And I saw you take her, and I followed you home. Now hand her over, please."

"Ah," I said. "I think I can solve this misunderstanding." I dragged a crumpled twenty-pound note from my back pocket. "I'll keep Slinky, my beloved pet of long-standing, and you take this, and get another cat."

"Twenty pounds?" he yelled.

"Hey, if you're proud, I can respect that. We'll go halves. A tenner each."

Sounded fair to me, but what I hadn't counted on was that the phrase *get another cat* turned out to mean "Why don't you stick this in your ear and twist it?" in Dr. Lane-language. Must have done, I reckoned, because Lane was really horrified.

"Get another cat?" he gasped.

I don't know if you've ever been to one of those weddings where everybody keeps throwing up on the bride's mother? But if you have, then picture in your mind the expression the bride's mother was wearing by the end of a long day, and you'll know just how much disgust one face can be made to contain.

"You obviously know nothing of cats, Mr. Potter, or you would realise that when one loses one's cat one doesn't just go out and buy another one."

"Sure," I said. "I can understand that. I'll tell you what, how about a *dozen* cats? Hey, think about it: if dry-cleaners took compensation that seriously, they'd all go out of business, right?"

He looked at me as if I'd just escaped the noose on an insanity plea, and marched out of the house, down the street, without another word.

"Seriously, Dr. Lane," I called after him. "I'm not kidding! I know where I can lay my hands on more cats than a faith-healer in a violin factory!"

So, OK: when I got home from the pub two days later to find one of my ground-floor windows broken open, and the house doing a neat imitation of a Slinky-Free-Zone, it wasn't exactly a three-pipe puzzle.

But, honestly. All that fuss over a cat? After all, Lane didn't know how much Slinky was worth.

I had about three hours before Carl arrived to take the portfolio which, with any luck, would keep me in sunshine holidays for the next three winters.

"Should've called you Lucky," I told Slinky, as I stuffed her back into the sack which, by now, was becoming like her second home. "I never thought nasty old Dr. Lane would be idiotic enough to let you out to play on the allotments so soon."

Which was when Dr. Lane, approaching unobserved from the rear, slammed his fist into my spine, shouting: "You moron! You've no idea what you're interfering with here!"

What I had no idea of, was why a grown doctor should be willing to assault a virtual stranger just to keep possession of a gingery cat with a kinky tail. What I did have an idea of, however, was that Lane had a big stick in his hand, and was just about mad enough to use it on me, as I lay sprawled at his feet. His grey face was red now.

On an impulse, I swung the sack, Slinky and all, right into his belly. The cat screamed; he didn't. He just tripped, fell, and landed with a splash in the shallow river. A splash and a thud, the latter caused by the sudden connection of his head with a rock.

I stared at him for about a minute. He didn't move.

I was still a little shaky when Carl arrived, but the vodka was helping.

"Where're all the other cats?" he asked, as I should have guessed he would.

"Who knows where staff go on their afternoons off?" I replied, haughtily. "To the pictures, I expect."

Carl laughed (which used up about ten minutes of the day, right off), took his photos, and eventually left. Slinky had chili for dinner. I had vodka.

When a noise in the hall woke me the next morning, I thought for a moment it was one of Slinky's old mates, discovering how to enter a house through the letter-box. But it was the local paper, with a stop press item announcing the suspicious death of Dr. Reginald Lane, 54, research scientist, at his home in River Walk.

At his *home?*

Police were said to be unable to explain why, when found dead, sitting in a sun-lounger on his veranda, Dr. Lane (who had been shot twice in the lower body at short range) was wearing wet clothing and had a crude, apparently self-applied, freshly blood-stained bandage on his head.

The mystery—for me—only lasted until the lunchtime TV news, which reported that an animal rights activist had confessed to the "justified execution of a mass-murderer." Lane had been right; I'd had no idea what I was interfering with.

Far from being an aggrieved pet-lover, the Doctor was actually what that Sunday's tabloids called a vivisectionist. Slinky —and all the other cats on the allotments —had been part of an experiment, a deeply illegal experiment, it transpired, designed to develop a rapidly contagious, but easily contained feline disease.

Quite who was sponsoring Lane's alfresco laboratory has never been established, but speculation centred on the government, on the property developers, on all the usual suspects. At any rate, some people, it seems, do not value urban feral cat populations in quite the way that I have come to value them.

And I certainly do value Slinky. I do. The calendar— *Slinky's Big Year* (text by J. Potter)—will be, Jenni's marketing colleagues assure me, the biggest-selling gift item nationwide, next Christmas. There is talk of an animated television series. Two book publishers are bidding for the rights to Slinky's autobiography, which I am to ghost-write (well, yeah, *obviously*). I'll have to make up some amusing adventures for her. The truth, I think, would not do at all.

Which brings me to why I'm writing this, strictly private, memoir.

The remaining allotment cats were rounded up by the council's vet, and taken away for tests "as a precaution." There was really no cause for concern, the authorities insisted, but just to be on the safe side . . .

(I bet they ended up on some health farm, all chili con carne and Ping-Pong and free booze, and all at the public's expense. While your average humourist has to virtually kill himself just to meet the mortgage. Ask me, the welfare state saps enterprise. Look at Slinky: she got herself a career, she didn't sit around waiting for handouts.)

I don't know if you've ever lived in close proximity to a cat which may or may not be carrying an unidentified bug, which may or may not be transferable to humans, and which may or may not kill you at sometime in the future? But if you have, then you'll know that it's something that tends to worry you a little.

But really, most of the time, I'm too busy worrying about what it's going to be like entering the super-tax bracket.

Still, "just to be on the safe side . . ."

If I should predecease my Aunty Cissie, I would like her to inherit my copyrights and royalties. And please, whoever reads this, tell her I'm terribly sorry I never visited her.

I'm not, in fact, but what I always say is: being nice doesn't cost anything, does it?

At least, it doesn't when it doesn't cost anything.

★ ★ ★ ★ ★

There is a sizeable market in the USA for crime stories involving cats, and I've written quite a few over the last few years. This was my first, originally commissioned in 1994 by Ed Gorman for an anthology he was then editing. It didn't, in the end, make it into that book, but appeared some years later in *Ellery Queen Mystery Magazine*.

In those days, I wrote stories very quickly—often in a single day—and without much forethought. I'd simply start off with an amusing snatch of dialogue, or an arresting opening line, and keep going until the job seemed to be done. With such a system, it's amazing that I ever sold anything—I can only suppose that, in some editors' minds, the liveliness of the writing was more important than the chaotic plotting.

A few years older, and somewhat more experienced at my trade, I couldn't write like that now even if I wanted to. Today, I prefer to pace myself, do a couple of pages here, a couple of pages there, eat regular meals—even sleep occasionally.

I'm glad to end my first collection with "Twelve of the Little Buggers;" I think it remains the funniest story I've ever written. Every now and then I re-read it, and it still makes me laugh out loud, immoderately and immodestly. I just hope I'm not alone in that reaction.

About the Author

Mat Coward was born in 1960, Kent and grew up in south Britain. He moved to London in 1978, where he worked for a year as a junior assistant at Merrill Lynch International Bank, then for seven years in public libraries. In 1995 he returned to Somerset, where he still lives.

He became a freelance broadcaster and writer in 1986, writing mostly humor columns and book reviews, but also a bit of everything else—scripts for stand-up comics, radio and TV, comic strips scripts, gardening columns, and anything else one might think of. In the late 1980s, he began reviewing crime fiction, which led naturally to writing crime short stories.

His first published story was short-listed for the inaugural Crime Writers Association Short Story Dagger (and he was an Edgar Nominee for another story in 2001). He's written dozens of stories (SF, horror, humor and children's, besides crime), and has been published in magazines and anthologies in Britain, the U.S.A., Europe, and Japan, and broadcast on BBC radio. His first book was a humor title, *Cannibal Victims Speak Out*, published in 1995. His first mystery novel, *Up and Down*, was published in 2000 to rave reviews and was followed by *In and Out* in 2001 . The third novel in the "Don and Frank" detective series, provisionally titled *Over and Under*, is scheduled for delivery early in 2003. When he's not writing, he generally spends my time gardening, watching or listening to cricket, or lying down in a dark room wishing he had a job that actually paid.